Paper Machete

Book Two of the
Emily Ellis Series

AMANDA JAEGER

Paper Machete

Editor: Genevieve A. Scholl
Cover Design: Troy Cooper
Formatted by: Genevieve A. Scholl

TABLE OF CONTENTS

Prologue 9
Chapter One 12
Chapter Two...22
Chapter Three...27
Chapter Four 37
Chapter Five...44
Chapter Six...48
Chapter Seven 56
Chapter Eight 66
Chapter Nine 74
Chapter Ten..84
Chapter Eleven..93
Chapter Twelve..101
Chapter Thirteen 110
Chapter Fourteen...117
Chapter Fifteen..123
Chapter Sixteen...134
Chapter Seventeen 139
Chapter Eighteen..146
Chapter Nineteen 154
Chapter Twenty..162
Chapter Twenty-One..166
Chapter Twenty-Two 173
Chapter Twenty-Three..184
Chapter Twenty-Four...190
Chapter Twenty-Five 197
A Review Request..9
About The Author 10
Acknowledgments..11

Family: A group of descendants of common ancestors
Family: A group of people united in criminal activity

Content Warning: Cult Activity

PROLOGUE

Noland

Bang.

Pretty sure that was the gas stove behind me, but I don't look back to find out. I don't have the luxury of glancing back into the fiery heat to observe anything I'm leaving behind me. I can only look forward. As I run up the stairs with extra weight in my arms, I hope against hope that the paintings I threw into the reinforced alcove are safe.

They should be safe. I built that area reinforced specifically to keep them safe.

Memento Mori *needs* them to be safe. Tucked away. Forever ready to be used for access to what I need.

I don't have time to check. I barely have the time to even think about what my next move is. All I can do is make my move instinctually, one foot right after the other.

Next step, next step, next step. Stabilize myself on the fourth step and race all the way up. Forget the door. There's no need to secure a secret door in the kitchen floor anymore. Not when *she* has decided to burn it all down.

This entire scenario brings a whole new meaning to Emily Ellis being a spitfire.

Smoke billows into the kitchen, like a black cloud ready to rain down on the two of us. A piece of me wants to watch which shape it'll form itself into. I want to know what it feels like to be in that cloud, feel it wrap itself around me and take me in, welcome me into a new plane of existence.

But I can't.

This isn't how I transfer over to the next realm.

I need *her* for that. And I need her talent to get us there.

I shift her dead weight in my arms. It's unbelievable how much she was willing to let go of. Her talent, her gift, and everything she knows as reality. And without even fully knowing how much she would be sacrificing. It's good I was there to keep her from wasting her future beyond the realm of reality.

Even if I wasn't able to harness her talent completely. Not yet, anyway. Not until I'm told I'm ready. And only then, will I have the support to do so under the watchful eyes of those who matter most. Her dead weight isn't dead. Just asleep. Resting. A tiny reddening sack of potatoes napping in my arms while I carry her out to a place more comfortable.

A hiss hits the floor behind me. Plastic and enamel bits have melted from the appliances and are creating little puddles around us. As much as the crackling and whooshing intrigues me, I can't stay here any longer.

We can't stay here any longer.

We need out. The world needs us out.

Fresh air greets us when I step outside. It takes everything within me to keep pushing my feet forward and away from the house. My lungs want to drink in the air around us, maybe even feed the same electrifying air to Mills in my arms, too. I can't figure out how to do that for her, though, so I let her unconscious body do it on its own.

And then I move. Quickly. Before anyone can see my face and question what's happened. As I run down the street, I realize that holding her in my arms feels like nothing. It feels like her weight was created specifically for my arms to carry. We turn the corner, onto a quiet side street away from where. No doubt, people will collect. They'll follow the smoke alerting them in the sky. They'll gape and gasp and throw their hands up to their mouths, wondering how something so tragic could happen.

Silly people. They don't know what real tragedy is.

There's a car waiting for me, with a man wearing linen behind the wheel. And right now, he has one job, and that's to take us to where Mills can get care.

Not just for the silly thing she did to our little house. Not just for the reddened skin on her face and hands. But for her heart. For her passions. I want to provide her with all the care she needs to better herself now, hone in on her talent, and allow it to allow us into our futures.

The man sitting in the driver's seat helps himself out, opening both doors on the passenger's side. "Memento Mori awaits, sir," he says with a smile.

I unload Mills into the back seat, sorry she's fainted, probably from a combination of smoke inhalation and shock. But I'm also not sorry that her decisions have made this part easier for me.

Before I help myself into the front passenger's seat, I zip my pants. I'm also not sorry that my emotions were cut short. They were getting away from me, and had I allowed them to take over with her — I take a peek at Mills asleep peacefully in the back seat — I would have ruined my own steps toward enlightenment.

Rules are rules. And now that I'm going back home with a recruit by my side, I can't risk breaking them. Life inside of MMS is far different than life outside of it.

"Let's go," I tell the driver. "To the commune, and the rest of our lives."

CHAPTER ONE

Mills

Pine needles and paste. I see nothing. I hear nothing. I feel nothing. My entire body feels asleep from the world and my consciousness. Somehow, it's my sense of smell that wakes up first.

Every bit of the scent creeps into my nose to burn the hairs inside and cling to what's left. I know, great image, right? My burning nose hairs seem to think so, too.

I'm sitting up.

I'm sitting up? At least, I think I'm sitting up, but my head feels a little funny. It's like waking up from the worst hangover ever, except I'm not hungry for eggs and starchy toast. My head pounds, my body feels numb, and I'm not sure I remember what happened last.

I am hungry for painkillers and understanding, but I'm going to go ahead and guess I'm not going to get either right away.

My legs move to stretch out from where I'm sitting. They want so badly to wake up their muscles and stretch their tendons, but they don't move. They stay in the ninety-degree angle they're in. And since my butt's sore and my shoulders are pinched back, I'm pretty sure I'm going to be stuck in this position for a while. I am tied to a freaking chair.

I blink my eyes open and instinctually try to rub the sleep out of them. Only, my hands don't move up to my eyes like I want them to. Of course they don't. I shift in the rock-hard chair hoping I can weasel my thin wrists out. But every time I move them, the rope or ribbon or whatever the heck is holding them back rubs against my sore hands.

My blurry eyes strain to focus. Where am I? Why do my hands and face feel hot when the rest of me feels cold? The blurry shapes in front of me start to focus. Who is this hooded figure standing in front of me and what is he doing?

He seems hunched over. His attention is on… what? A sink? I blink my eyes again, hoping they'll focus even more, and make more sense of where I am and what I'm doing here. While my sight works to catch up to my sense of smell, my brain works in overdrive.

Anything could be in front of that man. Anything at all. Poison to rot my brain away. Scalpels to cut me open. One of those metal claw thingies in sci-fi movies that will pluck out my teeth one by one to feed to some crazy monster. Depending on who that hooded figure is and why he has me here, I could be living out my worst nightmare.

Feeling nauseous, I pinch my eyes shut. If only I could remember what brought me here. Wherever here is.

Willing my nerves to calm and my brain to work, I tell myself to think.

Think hard, Mills. Get yourself together.

Orange and white light. For a moment, that's all I can come up with. Blinding light that took my breath away.

Breathe, Mills. Think harder. What else?

Sound? No sound? There was definitely ringing in my ears, which would explain why I'm struggling to hear anything coming from the hunched figure. Who knows what he could be banging together away from my sight. Maybe it's actually not as quiet as I thought. Maybe I'm temporarily deaf due to whatever that blinding light was. The thought makes my pits sweat. It seems like every tick mark is stacking up against me.

Breathe in and out, Mills. You're still here. You're strong. You've faced some horrible things in the past. Now isn't the time to lose yourself.

And then it hits me.

I open my eyes. The little bit of rest I gave them did them well because the hooded figure turns around. His eyes lock with mine, and every detail of those last moments comes flooding back.

Noland Elsinger's eyes that pleaded with me not to throw the lighter. His arm that reached out in a vain attempt to stop me, even though he was too far away. And right when I thought all was said and done, when all of his bullshit would be behind me, he ruined it. The last thing I remember is the feeling of his arms around me as he tackled my midsection. I guess he lifted me away and dragged me up the stairs. I guess they weren't as difficult to climb as I had thought.

Noland Elsinger, my art professor, Volga County's personal serial killer, and now my kidnapper dragged me away from the burning house and brought me here. Wherever here is.

"Oh, good, you're awake."

Oh, good, he speaks. And as he moves to the side, I realize he was working over a sink and bowl. Whatever is inside that bowl has my insides twisting and turning. A drying gloop on the floor makes me realize that, despite as pristine as this room appears, maybe these aren't floors to eat off after all.

"That's going to make the next bit so much, much easier."

Oh, good. There's a next bit. My burning hands dampen even more. I wish I could read his mind. Then my brain would know what to worry about instead of cooking up fear scenarios of its own. Waterboarding. Poisoning. Bodily torture, one fingernail at a time.

"You should be dead, Noland."

The explosion was supposed to end it. It was supposed to end *him*, and I was happy to go up in flames to make that happen. But he's a stupid cockroach that somehow survived a personal nuclear war aimed directly at him. If he could survive that, then I have no idea how I'm going to bring him down from whatever disgusting act he has planned with that goo in a bowl and me tied to a chair.

He gives me a nod that makes my stomach churn. "You sure tried your best, Mills. But you know, I built that place knowing every way in and out, and lucky for us, I was able to save both of us from that nightmare. It's just a shame I couldn't pull out the last paintings that were left behind, too."

The paintings. We were in a basement of fire and he was busy thinking about the two paintings he forced me to create. As weak as it feels, I muster up the snarkiest smile I can come up with. At least he wasn't able to take those from me. They died in the fire the way he was supposed to. The only aspect of those that I'll miss is the portrait I made of my best friend, Livvy. The string around my heart tightens just thinking about her.

"So glad to see you smiling, Emily Ellis."

My insides scratch together upon hearing him say my full name.

"Because you've probably already realized there was no way I was going to let those paintings be harmed in any way. I know every inch of that house and every millimeter of that basement. As long as they were slid into that little protective alcove, they'd survive a nuclear threat." He mimics my smile right back at me. "You'll get to reunite with those canvases soon, love."

Love? My skin crawls and prickles. Another tick mark has stacked up against me, and I have no idea how I'm supposed to break out of this nightmare to get back to the reality that was supposed to happen.

Where he is gone, I'm free, and Livvy never died.

I swallow back the burning sensation I feel creeping up in my throat and take in my surroundings. Minus the working goop-bowl, this place really is clean. The tile floor nearly shines and the walls are so white, I can almost see the glisten of lingering wet paint. If it weren't for the pungent smell of pine, I'm sure I'd be able to smell the paint still drying, too. There is only one thing that's hanging on the wall: a small painting, a single art piece that makes this place almost feel welcoming. It's a proud man standing under a tree with a machete in one hand. *Machete Man* by Puerto Rican artist Oscar Ortiz. How I wish I could hold that machete right now, feel the power it would give me, break out of these restraints, and finish the job I aimed to do before I was kidnapped.

My wetting palms try to break free again.

"Not comfortable, love?" Noland pats me on the head like I'm some sort of pet looking for comfort. I'm not. But I am looking for something. I want a way out. I want a way free.

As if he forgot all about our conversation about the paintings left behind, Noland turns back around to the paste bowl to keep mixing. And I focus on the other pieces of the room, hoping for a clue that will offer me a way out of this mess.

The bay window in front of me is decorated with hanging plants and gorgeous vases filled with every flower imaginable. Tulips, daisies, roses, and… well, I don't know what else because that's the extent of my flower knowledge. Guarantee, it's a lot. It's a regular Eli Halpin painting in real life. *Maybe that window unlocks. If I could get that window open, it wouldn't take much to jump out of it and run for my freedom, right?*

Outside the window shows me a field, green grass with those pretty little lawnmower lines. There's a giant pine tree in full display, and I wonder if what I'm smelling is actually coming from that. My eyes drift into the distance. There's a whole row of the same pine trees, so I guess it could be any one of them or the combination of all of them together. Just an entire land of built-in air fresheners over here. I wish the Machete Man were real, ready to stand under any one of those trees to swing his blade in all directions and let me out of this thing.

Then again, I don't know if any of the groundskeepers hard at work out there would actually lend me a hand… or if they would shove me back into this room, forcing me back onto this same chair, right where I started.

Then there's the thing that makes me even more uncomfortable. The bed. I gulp down a sour taste. The sheets are so thin, they look like they've been washed a thousand times over. And even if it hasn't been slept in recently, I'm afraid just the presence of it is enough to feed the creep in front of me ideas I don't want him to have. It's not like he hasn't tried to just grab whatever he wanted on the spot before. My *talent* as he called it.

My heart races at the way his echoed words ring in memory.

I try to pull my hands free again, but their sting is too much. There is no way I can slip out of whatever knot is back there. Not without skinning the burned flesh off my hands, and even then, I don't know if I could wriggle free.

"You don't have to worry about a thing, love," Noland tells me from over his shoulder.

Easy for him to say. My heart is doing its best not to slam itself out of my ribcage. I have everything to worry about.

"We'll get your paintings soon. I promise you, I'll have them in my hands in no time, and they'll be where everyone can view them, take in their brilliance. I promise you, I have all of that taken care of. I'd never let anything happen to them, love. Because we need them. You don't even know how important they are to our future together."

I wish I could close my eyes and open them back up without this man in front of me. I wish this was a terrible dream and I'd wake up in Joe's coffee, sitting across from Livvy, listening to her explain some kind of weird thing about beans that makes zero sense to me but would light up her eyes like magic.

But I close my eyes, open them again, and reality is still reality. I'm still stuck in this room with Noland, and Livvy's still gone. My heart hurts. For me. For her. And for her brother, Stark. I wish I could at least give him a hug, tell him I'm sorry, let him know that I did my best to rid her of her killer. But here I am, just listening to her killer verbally fondle my paintings.

"We'll get to them later, but for now, we have to prepare."

Each word he oozes out pulls on my skin to prickle up the hairs on my arms and neck. "Prepare for what, Noland?"

He cocks his head as if I should understand. "For the fine arts gallery and auction, silly. You've been working so hard to get in. We're not going to stop now." He makes his way over to me and kneels down on the floor.

There he goes again, digging into his pocket of goodies. Noland must have been a boy scout in a former life. Always prepared. And out pops… Vaseline. He never ceases to confuse and terrify me. Whatever he has planned is worse than pulling out my nails from the base of their beds.

"The gallery is only a week away, dear. We're putting together all the submissions now, and soon they'll all be ready for public viewing, where the entire county and beyond will come, have a look, and the higher beings will decide who gets to move forward from there." He squints at my face. "A little burn isn't going to stop us from going. We need to go, love. We need to attend and you need to be by my side."

I shake my head. "I won't go anywhere with you *by my side*." I nearly spit out the words, and when I hear how they sound against my ears, I recoil. Now probably isn't the time to be provoking a serial killer.

"Oh, but you will, dear. You will."

He unscrews the Vaseline lid and dips his four fingers inside the jelly. He scoops a handful out. It sits on his palm like an alien offering. Noland puts down the jar and inches closer, the glob in his hand becoming mere inches away from my face. If it had a smell, I would be gagging on it. I gag anyway. I don't want that near me. I don't want to feel whatever he has next in mind.

I try to move back in my seat away from his hand. I don't want him to touch me. The idea of it makes me want to crawl out of my own skin. But shifting my weight around in the seat I'm tied in is no use. There's no budging this thing and no matter how much I try to dodge his hand, it's there. In my face.

This is one of those times I wish I could experience things outside of myself.

The clear jelly slabs on my skin. If anything were in my stomach, it would work itself up and out and clear all over the floor. But I don't even know the last time I ate, and all I can do is dry heave because *this man is touching my face with petroleum jelly.*

Even though my head is less fuzzy and my sight is clearer, I still don't know what this means.

"Now, now, just stay still, love. We need to cover you up, but I don't want to cover your nostrils because then you won't be able to breathe. We can't have that, can we?"

I don't want to admit he's right, but he is. Even though there's a piece of me that wants whatever is going on to end, no matter what the price, there's still a bigger piece that feels the fight to keep myself alive. Because now that I know I'm alive and so is he, I need to stay that way so I can finish what I started. As terrifying as this all might be, Livvy and all the other girls aren't going to die in vain.

And as much as I don't want to admit it, the jelly on my face is actually soothing. Yup, I must have burns on my face, too. Great.

When he finishes slathering under my chin, he wipes both hands on his linen jumpsuit — *linen jumpsuit* — leaving greasy stains where his fingers trailed. I wish I could shake the goo off of myself, too. I wish I could shake like a dog and cover him all over with the residue I did not sign up for.

But then he goes over to the sink and dips his hands into the bowl of smelly gunk and pulls out a long, wet strip of newspaper. No; not newspaper. This doesn't have any writing all over it. This is a different paper, perhaps one specifically designed for this purpose.

What is this purpose?

Then it clicks. That's what he was doing over there. Making paper mâché. My heart flips down to the bottom of my stomach. How. Freaking. Creative.

"Now, hold still," he tells me, "because I don't want to block any airways. I promise I'll be gentle. All you have to do is relax."

Relax. Sure. Super easy to do, bud. I'd be surprised if he didn't see my hands shaking in their restraints.

And before I can do any kind of protesting, the cold, wet paper is on my face. I gag at the slimy feeling because I did not want this. I did not ask for this. I haven't been dying to be a part of this weird art project he has going on, and yet, I'm forced to sit here and endure it.

Another wet piece hits my skin, and I gag again.

"Sit still," he reminds me. But I can't help it. If there were anything in my stomach, it wouldn't just be all over the floor. It would be all over his face. I kind of wish I could make that happen.

Another strip goes on, and I can feel them crisscrossing each other. I can feel them building on top, creating a slimy mask on top of my face. And it hits me as he uses his fingers to flatten everything down. That's exactly what he's doing. He's making a mask of my face. He is literally replicating my face in paper mâché form.

Another hopeful wretch pulls up nothing.

"Now, now. Didn't I say don't move so much? We don't want to ruin the whole thing, love. Then, we'll have to start all over. You know I don't like to go back to square one on projects. It feels like such a waste."

Even if I had the words to ask what the hell he means, he takes away my ability to ask them with a few swipes of his hands. Just when I feel like I am starting to stand on more solid ground, he takes away the little bit of power I have.

More wet paper strips slide over my lips. He pats them down, tracing my bottom lip with his finger. I swear I see him bite his, and my entire body clenches.

What is he going to do when my entire face is covered?

"Okay, Mills, just a few more minutes, and then we play the waiting game. Just close your eyes for this part, okay?"

I want to keep my eyes open. I want to know what he's doing. I want to gain whatever knowledge I can of this oddly immaculate room, because if I can figure out where the heck this place is, I can get out, find Stark, and figure out a way to, at the very least, knee this moron in the groin as hard as I can.

But I can't keep my eyes open because Noland is covering them. Another few strips of wet paper settle over my eyes.

It's all dark. Everything is dark. And all I have left is my ears. My heart and a heavy ball at the pit of my stomach.

"You're almost ready, Mills. You're almost ready for the presentation of your lifetime."

CHAPTER TWO

Noland

The door clicks behind me, and my body leans against it. My palm lingers on the doorknob. I did it. I finally did it. Granted, this isn't what I originally had in mind, but when your first plan falls to pieces, you do what you can to make a plan B that will still get it done. And my plan B was definitely a little more aggressive than it should have been.

But aggressiveness is what gets wins, so I'm okay with that. From day one, I was told if I wanted to be "in" then I needed to make it happen for myself. So, with Emily Ellis behind this door, tied up and waiting, I'm making it happen. For me, and for her.

For all of us, really.

Patience. That's one of the lessons I've been told I need to hone in on, so I'll be repeating it to myself over and over until it's ingrained in me. That's what I tell myself now, with my back on the cold door and a warm body waiting for me on the other side. Patience.

With a deep breath in, I push myself off and away. I'll come back in a few hours. She'll still be here. Even if I wait most of the day, she'll still be here. And however I find her when I come back will be a true testament to how she'll take to our society here, away from reality. I'm sure she'll have patience, too.

While I wait for the base of my new artwork to dry, I take a stroll. There's one person I want to check up on. I've had a taste of what his recruit can do, and I have a feeling this is the one piece of competition I need to worry about. Giving that duo a little rattle might be exactly what this rivalry calls for.

Besides a few workers quietly tiptoeing around to complete their assignments, the hall is empty. All the handlers are tucked away behind their own doors. I stop the fourth door down. It might be closed like the rest and just as quiet, but I know exactly who is behind it.

I knock.

I don't even wait for an answer before my palm reaches the doorknob and turns.

"Noland, hello." Jon doesn't even look up. He's expecting me just as much as I expected him. "I'm a little surprised to see you here." *Lies.* "I would have expected you to show up much earlier with as loud as your confidence has been." That's a little less of a lie.

The doorway supports my side as I arch my sight over his shoulder. Inside his hands is a complete mask. He's done with his. The only thing left is any finishing touches to make it his. To brand his recruit fully his.

"Well, I didn't want to bother you while you were busy." Really, I wanted to wait until he had something in his hand I could rattle him with. "I wanted to wait until I thought things were a little calmer in your room."

I'm a little jealous that his mask is almost done while mine is still slowly drying down the hall. Jon finally looks up at me. I hoped to see concern on his face, but it's not there. I see confidence. Cocky confidence.

"Then you came at a good time. Come on in, Noland. Have a seat."

He doesn't offer me an actual seat. He's not the gentlemanly host he should be. But I take the half-ass offer anyway. I help myself into the room and then to an empty chair at the table.

"I imagine you came here to throw me off my game, Noland." He's back to the mask, slowly moving the little brush in his hand in tiny strokes. "But you should know, everything is already set. All work has been turned in. All that's left is the final call. And that, my friend, is out of our hands."

"You have me all wrong, Jon. I'm only here for support. I want to be right there with you every step that I can." I want to watch over his shoulder every step that I can, too. Get close to the cage and shake its bars. "We are family, after all, right?"

He looks up at me. It takes a moment before he cracks a smile. "Family," he says. "That's right, brother. We are building a family. And I have a new sibling who fits perfectly in the family tree."

On cue, the bathroom door swings open and out comes a young blond man. As he looks up at Jon and myself, a nervous smile creeps out. "Hi?" He's a lost boy with rosy cheeks. Even his stature doesn't have an ounce of confidence. I can see exactly why Jon picked him up. He's the kind of artist who doesn't know what he has when he has it. He's the kind of artist that can be manipulated when needed.

He's the kind of artist who doesn't have the specialness that Mills has. Those bars are rattling again.

"Zak, I'd like to introduce you to Noland. He's another handler, just like me. He's here to support us as we build an artistic family together. He's a talented artist himself, so if you ever need any help, feel free to ask him, okay?"

Zak nods, but I'm not sure he's buying into the ingenuity dripping from Jon's words. Rattle. Rattle.

"You mean when we get to meet all the others? Will he help me not be so awkward around everyone else?"

Jon laughs. "I don't know if this is the guy you want friendship advice from." Then he refocuses his gaze on the work in his hands. "Besides, you'll do just fine, Zak. Everyone loves an eager buddy who's ready to show off his work."

I notice Zak's cheeks redden, turning him into a little cherub. Maybe Jon is right. Maybe this kid is ready to be a part of our family. He's ready to do good for our cause and become part of The Circle. I'd be proud for him if it weren't for the fact that he might knock me and Mills out of the way. And I just can't have that. Mills can't have that.

Jon lifts up the mask he was working on. It's plain. Extremely plain. Boring plain. Blank canvas plain.

"You're going rather safe with that, aren't you?" I ask him.

Jon frowns. "The Dignitary did say all recruits are clean slates until they're marked. I assumed they should appear that way until after judgment."

He's not wrong. We are all clean slates until judgment time. But I feel like as handlers, we've at least earned enough respect to help the image of our recruits where we can. Most things are completely out of our hands. But our recruits? That's our doing. We should have a say. We should get creative. Aren't some rules meant to be broken if they're for the greater good?

"Here." Jon holds out the plain white mask to Zak.

Zak takes it and blows on the last bit of still-sticky paint.

"Try it on," Jon urges. "Let's see what you look like."

He does. Zak slips the mask over his face, and it fits perfectly. A snug puzzle piece that overlaps its partner. When it's on without flaw, Zak looks just like a faceless doll, as if someone wiped his features away and all that's left is a blank canvas. A blank slate who hasn't been tagged and placed yet.

"Perfect," Jon says. "I think you're ready."

From under the mask, I imagine Zak's cheeks redden again. I imagine his smile is wide. I imagine his eyes are sparkling. His body language says he feels ready, and when he pulls off the mask, I'm right. His facial features say it, too.

"Now, now, put it back on. We're going to head out soon. Remember why you came here, right?"

"For the artistic expression of a solidary family."

"That's my boy."

That might be why these two are here. But I have my sights on the bigger version of that. And I'm going to do everything I can to make sure Mills stands out so we can do just that.

CHAPTER THREE

Mills

It's been an hour at least. Probably more. Time doesn't really make a lot of sense right now. It feels like forever since Noland left this room. I don't know where that cockroach skidded off to, but he left whistling a little tune right on out the door as if he does this kind of thing all the time. You know, kidnap a former student, tie her up to a chair, and force her face to become a mold for his newest paper mâché project. No big deal.

I guess for him, it's not a big deal. He's not the one stuck to a chair, bound and mute. He can move freely around. He can *choose* to do whatever the hell he wants.

So, I've been sitting here since, with my eyes and mouth damn near glued shut and my wrists and ankles tied around this uncomfortable wooden chair. My shoulders ache from being pulled around the chair's back, and my feet wish they could touch each other, instead of the individual wooden chair legs. There's no warmth in this thing. There's no care. Even though I've been sitting here for possibly hours, it's still just as cold and hard as if my body heat never touched it. Couldn't he have at least used a cushion?

Everything is falling asleep. My feet and hands lost that tingly feeling a little bit ago and now all I can feel in them is a little bit of numbed pressure when I try to circle my ankles or wriggle my fingers. I try to shift my position even more, and with the right movement, I do move the chair a little. But it's not enough to do any good. Even if I were able to push it over, I still don't think I'd be able to break free of these restraints.

Everything on top of my face feels tight and rigid. The paper mâché must be ready. Underneath, I'm thankful for the greasy barrier Noland slathered on me, even though I hate he had to get uncomfortably close to me. Even the thought of his touch makes my insides tense up and want to die. I can't imagine what else he would do with those hands if I allow him to get that close to me again. But at least my skin is a little soothed. It doesn't feel as hot and angry as it felt before.

And, hey, Noland also had the decency to leave me nostril holes, too. Hooray for tiny victories. No suffocation here today, folks.

Since the moment Noland left, I have adjusted my focus to my ears, trying to gather whatever auditory information I can. So far, I've noted a few things. One: there are several groundskeepers and they haven't stopped working. I've heard lawnmowers and leaf blowers coming from the window. Two: the air conditioning in here is freezing. And yet, I can barely hear it doing its thing. It's just me and the almost inaudible whirr in this room numbing me from my extremities inward. And, finally, there are definitely more people inside this building. When Noland opened the door, I could hear voices. Nonchalant voices talking chit-chat about lunch preparations and the weather. I have to wonder if they saw me at all. And if they did, then why didn't they say something? Why didn't they come and help? Isn't that what normal people would do?

Unless they're not normal people.

Unless they're in on it, too.

It. What *is* it, anyway?

Considering what Noland did to get here — murdering innocent girls to give me their hair to paint with — I can only imagine what might be considered normal. If he's capable of getting away with multiple murders, what have the hands of these other people done in the past?

What could they do in the future?

I hear voices again, muffled behind the closed door. I can't make out what they're saying. There are two, no, three different inflections. And laughter. There's definite laughter behind that door, but I can't imagine what anyone could be laughing about. I see nothing funny about where I am, what I feel, and what I've last seen.

I suppose that's confirmation that, at the very least, these people have a warped sense of humor.

Now, if I could get myself free, then I'm sure there would be something funny about my situation. At least there would be something hilarious about Noland's face after I'd knee him where it counts and have my own way with him and my tennis shoe.

The door clicks open, and the voices outside sound closer.

"I'll let you to it, Noland. You're going to need that time before we start introducing our new family members."

"Jon," Noland laughs, but I can tell he's not finding this conversation amusing, "you don't need to worry about a thing. I'm already set."

More strained laughter tickles my ears, and then the soft click of the door again. Guess there are no pleasant goodbyes in this place.

"How are we feeling in here?" I hear the soft scrape of another chair adjusting on the hardwood floor in front of me. I assume Noland is adjusting himself comfortably, and I assume his question is directed at me, even though he decided to use the plural pronoun… as if he cares much about how *I* am doing.

I don't answer. Not even with a nod or a head shake. He doesn't deserve a response. And I'm a little afraid of how he'll react to it if I do respond. Guarantee what I'd like to do doesn't match up to his own wishful thinking.

"Hmm, I think maybe you're ready for the next step, Mills." And then I feel his body heat near me. It radiates through my arms and chest and unhappily tickles my neck. I hate the feeling.

The tips of his fingers dance along the edge of this mask he forced on my face. When he taps the hardened material, I can hear it *click click click* and feel the vibrations against my jaw. I feel like his plaything he's captured just to dress up, and I wish he would just get this part over with. I don't want to be his doll. I don't want to be anyone's toy.

He slides his fingers under the edge of the mask and ever so gently peels it up. It's taking forever for him to wiggle it this way and that just to get it off. And now I'm wondering how much help the petroleum jelly actually did. Hopefully, the sting doesn't come back on my skin. Hopefully, pulling this off doesn't make it worse.

Hopefully, I don't see any pink flesh-colored pieces detach themselves, attached to the paper mâché when he pulls it off.

It comes off. My lucky stars, it comes off without any fleshy bits.

I stretch my jaw out and feel it pop, then blink my eyes into focus. The light in the room almost blinds me, it feels so bright.

"There we are," Noland says. He's nearly cooing at the piece of hardened plaster in his hands. "All set up. Just needs the finishing touches."

"What finishing touches?" I ease out.

"Ah, the pretty ones." He gives me a wink.

A lifetime ago, that wink would have had me eager putty in his hands. Now, it has my spine scratchy.

He opens up a cabinet above his head and shuffles around. Things from inside clink together as his hands move back and forth inside. After a minute or so of nothing but the clinky-shuffling sounds, he stops.

Knives? Needles? Or is he going more creative like he did with the line of girls from before?

Out comes a handful of pretty jars. They're cute little things, with fancy labels on the outside: Mahogany, Ballet slipper, Azure, Porpoise. All the frilliest names for colors you can possibly think of. Jars of paint.

Had I seen this anywhere else, I would be excited to dip into each one and test it out on canvas. Here? I don't know what on earth to possibly expect.

One more reach into the cabinet and he pulls out a paintbrush.

One with blonde bristles that match the end of my pigtails. It makes my stomach flip-flop.

But he turns around, with his brush in one hand and my face in the other. Not my face-face, but the paper mâché version, which somehow feels even more awfully intimate than the real thing.

"Now, I would typically ask you to handle this, but given your," he twirls the paintbrush around like a wand, "predicament, I think I'm going to handle this part myself."

"You mean given the fact that you kidnapped me and restrained me to a chair in what? A hotel room? That kind of predicament?" My nerves are getting the best of me, and they're making my mouth run without a second thought.

He shakes his head. "No, love. This is no hotel room. This is, well, it's a temporary home for now." He leans down to my level, and I take a good look at his face. He's a lucky jerk. His face looks clean. Smooth. Not even pink at all. It makes me even more sour at the fact that my hands and face both sting.

"We're lucky, you and I. Because in just a few days, we'll move on up to a more permanent location."

My nerves can't hold me back any longer. If I'm here, I'm here. And whatever he's going to do, he's going to move forward with it. No time like now to show him what my true feelings are. I rear back the spit in my mouth and spit it out. Bad aim strikes yet again. It lands on the floor. He ignores it. Of course he ignores it.

"But before we get there, we've got to do this." Noland stands up, smiles, and turns to the table that's next to me. Here, he sits down and places the mask and brush in their place. A quick rearrangement of the table, and all the paints are lined up, too.

I do my best to keep my voice from showing any shake. "Noland, what the hell do you mean we have to do this? Why do you have my face in your hands? Why do you have me tied to this stupid chair?" I try to move in place and the chair shifts just slightly. Again, another reminder that as much as I'd like to get out of this position, it just won't let me.

"Calm down, Mills. You have nothing to worry about."

"That doesn't answer my question, Noland. And judging by where I stand, or rather sit, I think I have plenty to worry about." I shift the chair again, but it only moves a hair. What's more apparent is the cold, edgy sweats forming under my arms.

Meanwhile, Noland is cracking open jar lid after jar lid. He dips the brush into the white jar. Oh, sorry, I mean the *alabaster* jar. And starts going to town on my paper face. With each little brush stroke, I can almost feel the bristles on my own face.

"Relax, love. All you need to know is that in a few days, we'll be as good as gold to the next steps of life. I'll be standing in The Circle, ready to make way for the new realm and you'll finally be able to live out your purpose."

He wipes off the alabaster from the bristles and dips it into a crepe-colored pink. The end of the brush makes two little circles on the closed eyelids. My own eyelids twitch in response. Vacant eyes on my paper face stare back into mine.

The blonde bristles turn dark when he dips it into the rosewood jar. With careful precision, he makes two swift little lines to create a painted mouth. Closed off to words and ideas. Shut tight to keep them locked away from the world. My own mouth pulls tight. I don't want my words taken away.

Another clean off, and those same bristles turn azure blue, and he goes right for the eyes again. Only, instead of irises, which would be the normal person's thing to paint, he paints in butterflies. I remind myself, Noland isn't normal, so this makes sense. Butterflies, just like the butterfly in my last painting. The one of me. The trapped one. Ugh.

I have no idea what he means by The Circle or what he's going to do standing there in it, but I'm feeling like I'm being taken for a ride I never asked to be on, and my insides are turning inside out.

"Noland, in a few days? Do you mean the art gallery?" After everything we've been through and everything he's put me through, it's hard to believe he's still concerned about an art gallery.

He holds up the wet mask and puckers up his lips to blow on the paint. After a few moments, he spins it around and I see my painted face staring back at me. It's like looking into a death mirror.

"That's exactly the point, Mills. You're going to be on display, too."

My eyes shoot open. Display? And what in the actual hell does that mean?

"Oh, calm it, Mills. We all are. It's what the gallery is all about. All of us. Together. Ready to be taken, accepted, and granted the next space with our names on it."

Just then, there's a knock on the door. My neck hurts when I strain around to see who might be there as Noland goes to answer it. Maybe it's someone who can help me. Maybe it's —

"Hi Jon."

Oh. Great. Maybe it's the same guy Noland was just in the hallway laughing with.

Only this time, I can see him. He's stout, balding. He looks like a high school janitor without any ambition in his life. Yet, here he is, locking eyes with Noland.

And next to him is someone else. Someone I can't see because they are wearing a painted mask on their face.

"Are you about ready for transfer, Noland?"

"Just about. You go on ahead. We'll arrive fashionably late."

Jon shakes his head. "Don't let the Dignitary find out."

"I'll be fine, Jon. Once she sees my recruit's talent, a few minutes won't make a difference."

Recruit. Talent. Dignitary. These men are talking in circles. The Circle. I'm tossing all these words in my head like spare change in my pocket. Individually, I know what they are. Together though?

"Suit yourself, Elsinger. We'll see you there." Jon grabs hold of the masked person next to him and leads them away by the arm. I suppose wherever they're going, we'll be going there soon, too.

Noland waves, smiles, and drags that smile back to me. "Emily Ellis, we're going to get you ready."

His hand touches my arm, and as much as I don't want that, I'm relieved. Because that hand travels backward to my hands. Before I can even talk my skin out of crawling, the pressure in my wrists loosens. My shoulders relax. The pain in my neck decreases. And for the first time since I woke up in this place, my hands are untied.

I work my fingers, hoping to ease them out of the numbed state, but a few shakes don't even wake up the blood flow. My hands open and close, hoping I feel that pinpricking feeling soon.

While I'm waiting for that feeling to kick in, Noland bends down at my level and inches closer to my face. "You trust me, Mills, don't you?"

Before all of this, I would have answered without skipping a beat. Of course I could have trusted him. He wasn't just my professor. He was my mentor. He was the one person who understood me and the one person who believed in what I could create with my hands.

But now? Now I can't trust what his hands are capable of. And his request to do so has me more on edge than any questionable frat party ever had in the past. That includes the hooded fingers dancing on the Greek lawns.

He nods, as if I answered, then he goes to work on my ankles. First, he takes the ties off my left foot. It feels like freedom. Like I could run out the door and escape out of this hellhole. But when I try to move it, my foot sinks like lead back to the floor. They're still numb, too.

I don't even notice my right foot is untied until Noland stands up to assess my stance. My eyes look up. From here, he looks like a giant. He looms over me, with a jeering smile that makes him appear so freaking proud of what he's done.

"You trust me, right, love?" he asks again, but I can't answer him. If I say no, his anger will rise to the surface. He'll go back through that little cabinet of his and find something that really will torture me. He'll get creative with scalpels and scrapers, and I won't have enough fight within me to walk away.

And if I say yes? His response may be even worse.

I can't move. I can't stand. Even if my nerves would, my feet won't allow it. I know if I even try, I'll end up flat on the floor with a broken ankle or two.

The whole situation is shit, and everything in my body knows it. Even the fibers in my hair.

He bends down over me. My nose picks up his breath, and even though there isn't a smell, the idea of the air that exited his lungs entering mine makes me choke on the breath I just took. One of his arms slides behind my back and the other underneath my thighs. The shock of his move triggers my fight or flight response. And at this moment, my gut reaction is to fly. I move my body as much as I can. I shake my arms and legs. That pinprinkling sensation I was hoping to wake back into my extremities comes shooting through my fingertips and toes like knives. It hurts. I scream.

And his arms catch me from falling off the chair.

"Tsk, tsk. You should trust me, love."

That's when I realize I made the wrong choice. Because I chose to show my mistrust in my actions, the look in his eyes darkens. He's got something planned for me, and it's going to be worse than what my imagination could come up with on its own.

CHAPTER FOUR

Noland

Despite her attempts at kicking and squirming, I know the girl in my arms, my Mills, my love, understands me. Deep down, she holds trust in me. She just doesn't want to show it. That trust has been there since day one when I welcomed her into my classroom. It's been there when I held her hand through learning how to perfect her brushstrokes and through holding her hand in learning color theory. She's accepted my hand every moment she could. But baby birds have to fly. Sometimes, even earlier than they are allowed. I'll still offer her my hand, just like I did from the first day she became my student.

Actually, it's been there since before that. Since the moment I read her application to study and wrote her name on the list of students I personally recommended to attend Volga University.

So, this whole flailing thing? That's just for show. Silly girls always trying to fight off their help when they don't mean it.

"I told you, just trust me, love. This is a necessary step, and they're all waiting for you. So once you're done here, we'll finish up and go. You'll get to see what's been waiting for you all this time." I wait to see what her reaction will be. I'm hoping for excitement, but if excitement lives within her, it doesn't reach her eyes. That's okay. She'll see soon enough. I give her a smile. A wink. Maybe I can ease that excitement out. "I dare say, you might even have some fun with what's waiting." Nothing. Damn.

My arms tighten around her in an attempt to loosen her muscles. I want her to melt into me. I want her to feel how much I care about her and her talent. She should know how much she means to me, to *us*.

Perhaps the cleansing will help her see it all. It's a good thing I thought about that in advance.

I carry her past the cabinetry with the little kitchenette and push open the door to the bathroom. The air conditioning is set to sixty-five degrees, but the bathroom feels like it's dropped several below. Perfect.

Almost perfect.

The ice I left in the tub for her is slightly melted. I had hoped it would stay more solid. The more solid it is, the more she'll be able to cleanse herself of the banal world we're leaving behind, and the more she'll be able to welcome her new family with open arms. But I guess a little water never hurt anyone.

I place her down on the toilet seat. Comfortably. I don't want her to feel unwelcome.

When I straighten up my stance, I block the door. Not intentionally. It's just how the room is designed. Just enough space for two people. Her, sitting in front of me and me standing by the door to watch over her. Protect her.

My bottom lip tastes salty. I must have bitten into it while considering the next piece. Because I know what I'm about to ask her to do will sound impossible. I'm not a monster, I understand the hesitation she's bound to hit me with.

"Mills, everyone is waiting for us. But they can wait a few minutes longer. It would be best if you're cleansed first."

Her eyes shoot from the iced tub to me. They're saucers as she asks, "Cleansed? In *that*?"

I let out a sigh. Even though she's letting out a little bit of spunk, I feel like I've lost some of it since she woke up. Hopefully once she realizes how important she is to us, that fire will come back. I just know she'll use it to create what we need and spread the messages the world needs to hear. That's the kind of fire we run off of. That's the kind of drive that will save us all.

"Mills, I know it's hard to understand, but you've been living in a world that doesn't appreciate the messages it needs to hear. It's full of people who run their lives on nine to five workdays and with the importance of a dollar. But you know better than that, right? I know I taught you better."

She pinches her lips as if to tell me that she, in fact, does know. She just isn't going to say it out loud. It's okay. I know her well enough to understand her nonverbal language.

"Remember, Mills? Remember how we'd spend time in class talking about how important it was to address the things that are in your heart? To allow the world to see you for who you are? To let your vulnerabilities on paper so you can reach people in their own hearts?"

"I remember you telling the class how important it was to you." The cold must be getting to her, because her inflection is a little weird when she tells me this. But it can't be sarcasm. Art is serious. And what we do here is serious. This is part of my teachings, and not just in the college classroom.

"My point is, all of those ideas? The ones where we place importance on numbers and statistics and mechanical thought processes? The ones where we skip over the importance of who we are at our core? Those ideas don't belong here."

Those pursed lips again. She's also wringing her hands. I wonder if the reddened skin on them still hurts. I make myself a promise to help her with that, and the marks on her face. When I asked the doctor for something that will both ease her pain and heal her skin, he was eager to help.

In fact, he had a jar ready to hand me, as if he had planned it before I even asked. That's how amazing this place is. That's how prepared we are. At least how prepared we should be. Clearly, I'm running late on my tasks. And who knows how The Dignitary will react if I keep her waiting for too long. I don't want to end up on the list of non-Circle members.

So I turn around to face the door and swallow the concern building up.

"Strip." I know I sound curt, but I'm giving her the privacy I know she wants. Even hearing the word in my own voice, I feel everything within me clench. I have to focus on the wood grain in the door so I don't turn around and watch.

I don't hear her move, so I say it again, "Mills, strip."

"No way in hell are you going to get me in a tub full of ice." Her voice sounds shaky, which tells me she will get into it, with the right finesse of words

"Mills," I hold my tone strong, "don't think of it as a tub of ice. Think of it as an opportunity."

"An opportunity for what? To become a popsicle?" Her spunk is still tainted with shaky words. And it makes me even more excited to see where all of this goes.

"It's an opportunity to shed the ideas of the banal world and cleanse yourself into what we can offer here."

I take a peek over my shoulder. She's still dressed in her black t-shirt and worn jeans. And those lips are pursed again. I want to grab those lips and do unspeakable things to them, but I can't. And the fact that she's not budging means even more of our time is being eaten up. Jon and his recruit are probably already sitting in the paper room. And the rest of the handlers are probably feeding in their recruits one by one. We need to be there, but I need to make sure Mills is clean. Ready. Willing. She can't bring in any of the impure thoughts from outside.

I close my eyes and face forward to the door again. "I can see that you're hesitant. I understand that. Anyone in your position would be. But let me assure you, in a few days, you'll look back at this and be grateful. I know I was when The Dignitary first brought me in." A chuckle escapes me when I relive the memory. "Granted, that was much different from this. Then, it was all ten of us together. And we had to watch each other transform in front of our eyes."

When I pause, I can hear her suck in a gulp of air.

"I watched every woman chatter her teeth and every man shrink his parts to non-existence. We were all there. We were all a part of it. It's how families evolve, going through the changes together, and rising from them better and stronger.

"Love, I want you to be better and stronger, too. So when I say strip, know I'm offering you that chance. I won't look. Not if you cooperate."

"And if I say no?" Her challenge is so very weak. She wants to be a big badass fighter, but even her gumption knows this isn't what we're fighting for.

I swallow down the tiny amount of guilt creeping up my throat. I don't want to force her. I don't want to have to put my hands on her and make her go in. But if I have to, then I'll do anything for the good of the cause. "Mills, you have two options. You can strip and help yourself into the bath on your own. Or, I can help you if you need the extra encouragement."

I look over my shoulder again and see the contemplation on her face. If I know her well enough, I know which option she's going to choose. She locks eyes with me. They say, "Don't touch me." And when I turn all the way around to offer my helping hand, she says it with her mouth. "Don't touch me."

Bending to her level, I can feel her quick breaths. She's excited. She's ready. She's just a little nervous, which we all are during our first time.

I lay a hand on her knee and will it to stop shaking. "Do you need my help? I'll be gentle."

"Don't. Touch. Me," she says again. And when she does, she enunciates each word as its own sentence.

My fingers have a mind of their own, though, and they creep up to the loose ends of her shirt sleeve. I give it a little yank. Unfortunately, it doesn't budge.

She does, though. She yanks right back. "Noland, get your hands off."

A tear rolls down her cheek. She's sad. She's sad because she knows what's needed and sometimes, those things you need to do are hard. She's sad because the rest of her life is waiting for her, but she has to jump into the burning cold in order to reach it. I stand up and nod at her. I understand that sadness. And I understand what's waiting for her beyond it. I'd love to kiss it away, drink in her tears, and allow the newness to roll in on her. But as dry as my mouth is as it craves her salty tears, I don't act on it.

See? Patience!

"Like I said, I'll turn around. Ten minutes. That's all you need. For ten minutes, wash away everything you were ever taught and I promise, we will welcome you to your new life, full of artistic expression and support in how you want to conduct yourself. Ten minutes and I promise you, we will be out of here."

Her facial expression changes. It softens, just enough for me to know she's ready to face her nerves and try. A moment lasts forever as she contemplates her next move, and I realize I need to give her permission. That's usually how it goes; girls need permission to say yes to the things their subconscious says no to.

So, I turn around again. Face the door. Focus on the wood grain. I didn't notice before, but this section in front of my eyes makes a little 'x'. It's faint, but it's there. Another piece of proof of the perfection that is Memento Mori. It was put there for me. X marks the spot. The spot I need to focus on so my recruit can do what she needs, so she can wash away the banal. And I must focus on it so my body doesn't react to what's happening behind me.

A metal *clink* sounds from the floor. Her jeans are down.

X marks the spot. Focus on the X.

And within a moment, she gasps and sucks in the air around her in a high-pitched squeal.

The X. This is the spot.

The *tink tink tink* of cubes hitting each other tells me that she's sliding in. The X in front of me morphs. It parts. It makes way for two sleek legs and a torso. It forms a little pool for a Mills-sized form. It engulfs her in a way I wish I were allowed. More tinks. A little slosh. A few whimpers.

X marks the spot. Here. My spot. Our spot.

My body reacts when I hear her cry out yet again.

X. X. X.

Hang on, Mills. It's so worth it in the end.

CHAPTER FIVE

Mills

I'm not even sure where the blanket comes from. All I know is that it's around me. It's plush. Soft. And after the shitshow I was just in, this is a welcome cocoon. I feel like it's petting me, rubbing my raw arms back to life.

It's a bizarre feeling. Going from numbness to pin prickles, to frozen back to numbness.

I've been cold to the core since I've been here. But now, being out of that frigid soak, I realize whatever I was complaining about before was stupid.

That wasn't cold. Comparatively, that was a comfortable Spring day.

And now? I've got the warmth of summer. My entire body literally thaws into the blanket, my muscles start to melt. And when my eyes adjust yet again to my surroundings, I realize why it feels like I'm being rubbed down by a generous pet.

Noland has me in his arms. And I really am cocooned in this wonderfully plush, comfortably warm gift from the Gods.

Okay, maybe that's a little overambitious, but that's exactly what it feels like. My eyes meet his. They're kind. Caring. And even though my skin was crawling before, now it's welcoming this touch.

He's saving me from myself.

From my — what did he call it? — cleanse. Not sure I buy all that yet. Cleansing from the banal. What does that even mean?

Maybe it doesn't even matter. Maybe all that matters is the fact that he's here. He's warming me up. And his hands aren't roaming under the blanket at all.

Thank. Pablo. Picasso.

He smiles. I don't smile back. I don't know if I'm supposed to. I'm not even sure why I slid myself into that ice bath to begin with. I suppose it's because the sooner I did, the sooner I could get out. I didn't want to keep on fighting with a man who wasn't putting up a fight. I didn't want to poke the bear that had already been prodded to nearly shove me in that ice bath in the first place.

"Are you ready for transfer, Mills?"

My teeth chatter. "I'm ready to get the hell out of here, if that's what you mean." As in out of this blanket. Out of this bathroom. And back into my clothes where at least I'm covered.

He shakes his head, but his kindness is still there.

"Transfer it is." He pauses for a moment. "I tell you what." And another pause. But this time, I feel a bear hug that keeps my teeth in their place. Chattering is at a stop. I'm back to normal.

Well, as normal as can be for being naked in a blanket in the arms of a man who… well, I'm not so sure what to call him anymore.

"Let me put you down here. I think you're probably safe to stand up. And I'll give you some privacy. You can go ahead and slip back into your dry clothes and meet me right outside the door."

And just like that, he's out the door. He actually places me on the floor like a weak kitten and leaves me.

No time like the present to assess the damage.

I pull up one knee to my chest, then the other. Then, I wrap my arms around both knees, hugging them to my chest. My own body warmth is thankful for the blanket Noland gave me. It's even more thankful for the care he gave me.

He's right, too. I have feeling back in nearly every corner of my body. Wriggling my toes and fingers, I can even feel the pink burns coming back. Not in a terrible way, but it actually feels good. Like I'm alive.

Thank freaking goodness I can feel my burned fingers, because that means I'm alive!

And since I'm alive, that means I'm capable of doing anything. I can stand up where I am, and I do. I can climb back into my underwear and clothes, and I do. I can be grateful Noland asked me to shed them so I have dry clothes to wear, and I am.

And I can ride this wave of who knows what is happening all the way through. And I will.

The doorknob turns and I let myself out. Noland, like promised, is waiting for me. And he has my mask, my face, in his hands. I don't like this death mirror.

"I think we need to put something on that, first. Don't you?"

My confusion must be displayed on my face, because he laughs - *laughs* - and then points to it. Then I realize what he means.

"Don't want it to get infected, do we?"

My burns. Throughout all the cooling and warming and numbing and flip flopping, I kinda forgot about them even being there. But now all I can think is I wish he would have thought about that before he covered me with gooey Vaseline earlier.

Back into the cabinets he goes, but this time it's full of creams and solutions. Not art supplies, but medical supplies, which makes me wonder what kind of place actually provides both.

He pulls out a bottle of aloe, green goopy stuff that I never liked to touch as a kid. And then he pulls out another jar. This one is different. Clear liquid sloshes around on the inside and there's no pretty label to mark what it is. Comparing this jar to all the others with printed out, lushly decided names, the kid's song goes through my head, "*One of these things is not like the other.*"

Then a *third* jar shows up from the cabinet. What is this place? A supply store for all things jar related? But this jar is empty, which can only mean one thing.

Noland opens the aloe jar and he opens the unmarked jar. And using the empty one, he slops out some of the green goop and some of the unknown substance. He uses the handle of the paint brush to stir it together, then flips it around to dip the bristles back in.

I sure hope somewhere when I wasn't looking that he cleaned off all the paint because now he's painting the inside of this creep mask he made — the mask of my face — and I'm ninety percent sure I know exactly where it's going.

Once he has slathered the mixture all around the underside, he looks at me, smiles, and leans back in. "Here," he says. "This will help cool your skin. Make it feel better. Heal. And then you'll be ready for transfer."

"Transfer?" I ask, this time out loud.

"Transfer," he says as if that's an actual answer.

The mask feels cool against my skin, and even though I always hated the texture of aloe, I'm thankful for it. Everything goes dark as the mask is secured against my face, and a few minutes goes by. A few more. Then I lose track of time. Before I know it, my head feels light and I'm on my feet, being pulled by the arm to somewhere for *transfer*.

CHAPTER SIX

Mills

My feet are moving, but I don't really feel them. They're just kind of dragging along as if they know what to do even though my brain doesn't have a clue.

I hear voices. People shooting the breeze around me, but I can't make out what they're saying. The words aren't clear. I don't even know how many people are talking. Their voices all mix together as one muddy sound that trickles into my ears and sticks there.

My head feels airy. Light. It's kind of that feeling between falling asleep and waking up.

A bed would be so nice right now. I'm so tired. The bed in that room. The room… wait. I'm not in it anymore, am I? There's no way Noland would allow me up from the chair to get into bed. No; he's taking me somewhere where…

Transfer. That's the word he used, right?

Why are my thoughts so broken? Maybe my thoughts are as tired as my brain. And body.

And my feet. They're still part of me, right? I think so. I picture them dangling at the bottom of my legs, and yet somehow they're still bringing me to…

To where? I hope there's a bed. A place to lay down. A place for my brain to unfog and…

Who do these voices belong to? And why can't they untangle them so I can understand?

Maybe they're not tangling their voices at all. Maybe it's my brain doing it for them. It's tying them together in a fantastic knot that I'll never be able to undo. Ha. My brain. I picture it with tiny arms grasping at foggy voices and frantically tying them together.

Oh shit.

Whatever Noland put on my face.

I think I'm drugged.

A force pushes my back, ever so gently, and my body moves forward, almost in slow motion. Maybe it really is in slow motion. I don't know. But it moves and, somehow, I sense more people around me even though it's completely quiet. So quiet, I can hear the drumming of my heart. It's slow, too. The lub-dubs are more like lub … lub… dub.

I'm sitting now. I think something made me sit. Or someone? But I'm definitely not in the chair I was in before. I'm not even tied down! Yay!

It's the floor, though. At least, I think it's a floor. It's hard, cold, and pretty uncomfortable. But again, I'm not tied to anything so my tired brain rejoices in that. It does a little dance, wobbling up and down and… *calm down, brain*. I'm already dizzy enough.

I feel something move beside me. Warm. Soft. But then it stops moving. I wonder if whatever it is is as dizzy as I am. The same thing happens on my other side. Then, something warm is in front of me. The same something touches the sides of my face. It pulls away. Off goes the mask and I have to blink in the light again.

Noland is in front of me, holding my paper face in his hands. As he backs up, I look around me. Several other people are on the floor with me, and each one has another person leaned over, slowly taking off masks from their faces.

One by one, paper faces pop off the people around me and the people in front of me all back up, holding the painted replicas in their hands.

These people, the holders, ease their way around the cafeteria style tables in the middle of the room until they reach the wall across from us.

Now we're on display. I can almost feel a spotlight shining on us, waiting for us to stand up and perform some musical number or kickline to be judged on. Not that I would know how to do either. But I can feel their eyes looking us over and their hungry smiles drinking us in.

Wait, why are there cafeteria tables in here? My stomach growls, and I really hope that we can eat some food. Mac and cheese would be nice. Or spaghetti. Or even a hefty salad. I'll gladly eat some rabbit food if it's available. Anything to fill up my empty stomach.

My head does its swimmy thing again. Well, maybe once I can stand without help. Maybe then I'd be able to eat anything in front of me.

A door slams open and my eyes drift over to it. There's a woman walking in. She's short. With fiery dyed red hair. And…

Holy. Crap.

Cokebottle glasses. I remember this lady from the craft store, spitting all over me as she talked. Well, talk is a kind word for what she did. She more or less admonished me for living as "one of those darned kids."

So, here we are, in a room of tables and masks and all these people, with the cokebottle glasses lady.

And for some reason, everyone standing on the other side of this room is taking a step back. I think it's a step. My eyes see them all moving so slow, but I mentally count to one watching them move, so it must be one collective step.

And they're all turning toward her, as if ushering her into the room with more respect than Van Gogh himself. She walks in, clicking her feet on the linoleum floor. She steps onto the bench seat of one of the tables, then makes her way onto the tabletop itself.

She's standing there, larger than life, and all I can think about is how she's about to spit on the table she's standing on and how if those double doors to the left of the room open up with trays full of food, then

I'm going to sit anywhere but at that table, even if I have to drag myself, crawling on the floor to get there.

"Good day, ladies and gents."

Either whatever is in my system is easing out or this woman has been practicing her speaking voice at home because I can hear her clear as day.

"I want to welcome you to the Memento Mori Society. You are our honored guests. You have been chosen. You have been seen for your talents and hand selected with them in mind to be right here, in this spot."

Hand selected. My mind takes those words and sits with them. Hand selected. It plays with them, bouncing them back and forth in my dizzy head. Hand selected.

Noland had *hand-selected* me. Not for his own self-centered purpose, but for this — I look around, clear confusion on all the floor people's faces — whatever *this* is.

"You are probably wondering what you've been selected for," she continues.

And she's right. I would really like to know why I'm sitting on this cold floor with a handful of other *selected* people to sit right next to me. People I don't know. People who look just as confused and eager to know why the heck they're here, too.

"All I can say is that you have more talent than most. We've seen what your hands can do and what your minds can create. We know you have a passion for the art world, and we do, too. We would love nothing more than to hone in on *your* craft, help you improve what's already so amazing about your work, and help you share it to the world."

In a way, her words echo Noland's.

"We know there is nothing more powerful than the solid creativity that lives in your heart. Because it is that creativity that will absorb whatever message you have to tell the world and release it to its viewers when the time is right. We know that with your craft, you have the ability to move people. You have the ability to enlighten people. You and your craft can and will change the world, and we want to be a part of that movement.

"We are a family of artists who take our art seriously. As so, we also take your art seriously. We understand the pains you have taken to get here, regardless if you knew this is where you'd end up or not. We know it's been difficult. We know there are people in your life who have laughed at or downplayed your ability to move others. We do not stand for that. We are here to be your support. We are here to ensure your messages are received and preserved. We are Memento Mori, and we welcome you."

There are a few murmurs around me. A few excited murmurs, even. I can hear tiny happy voices excited about finally getting taken seriously and having the support they've always craved.

But I can't seem to muster up the same excitement. I mean, who could? I look over at Noland, who looks proud to hold my face in his hands. And the two sides of me — the one who wants to burn holes into him and run away and the one who wants to warm up to the hope that this place really is a supportive network of artists — are at war.

I glance over at all the others standing beside him across the room. They're all like that, too. They're all proud fathers and mothers looking at their children from across the room. Us. The baby birds who are still sitting in their nest refusing to fly at the word of the strange red-headed woman who just told us we were safe.

"So, it's like art camp?" a girl near me asks. She adjusts her position, getting comfortable with her legs underneath her. Her hair is red, too, but it hangs on her shoulders in lighter strands. It feels natural, just like how her words slip out. "This place? It's like art camp, right? You're like teachers who can help us learn? Help us push the creative envelope?"

"Yeah, that's what I was told," a boy in a red shirt chimes in. "That this is where we're free to break away from all the crappy expectations we've been given and do what we want. Artistic exploration and all that. But aren't we just kinda working toward the gallery?"

Before I know it, there are voices all around me chiming in, and I can hear them all clearly and precisely. They've all submitted artwork for the gallery. They're all ready to be presented. But even more so, they're all ready to play and explore with art. And they're ready to have the space and time to do so.

The woman standing on the table raises her hands to quiet the room, and just like magic, it works. When all the murmuring stops, she addresses us all. "Friends, you're currently sitting in the room filled with the best of the best. If you look around you, these are the faces behind the artwork you will see in the gallery. Get to know them. Get to know their names. Being here, with artists who are on your level, is going to help you challenge yourself and stretch you past your current limits. Each of you has a strength that perhaps someone else doesn't have. Learn from those hurdles so you can overcome others in the future."

She takes in a deep breath before she continues, "If you let them, the people in this room will support you unlike anyone else who might be in your life outside these walls. These are the people who get it — who get *you*. Because these are the people who have had similar struggles, desires, and goals. These are the people who understand the value in art and want to hold onto it with everything they've got. These people are you and you are they. We're in this together. The world needs us to perfect what we know and we need each other to actually make that happen.

"So, yes, you have each submitted art that is valuable to the art gallery, but you all know, and it's very clear, that the gallery isn't it. That's just the first step in creating something bigger, better, and more meaningful. It's just step one in being real serious about the thing you love to do. So, yes, the gallery is important, but it's not nearly as important as what comes after, including the goals you have set for yourself. So, please, let us and let the group around you support you, love you, and encourage you in a way no one else can. Because let's face it, no one else in this world has proven to have the mindset of a mastery artist that you can think of."

I am in shock. Awe. The last time I heard this woman, she was not nearly as well-spoken as now. It's like getting her in the middle of the room with an audience was exactly what she needed to find her voice and use it.

And use it, she did. Because everyone around me is slowly nodding in approval. "Yes," they say. "It makes sense," they say. "It's true. No one else actually gets it," they say.

But, is it true?

I swallow back the burning feeling creeping up into my jaw. Because Livvy believed in me. Even if she wasn't an artist, necessarily, she got me. And she supported me. She cheered for me even when she wasn't fully getting it. There's only one other person who got me like that. And he was my mentor. Then he turned into a freaking serial killer. Then, he turned into my…what? Caregiver? I hate this place and the confusion it gives me

Then, all of a sudden, Noland and the others standing alongside the wall all shift in unison. The woman on the table turns to address them to say, "Now is the time!" They all form a line and nearly march over to the double doors.

I'm praying for chicken nuggets, dino-style.

They enter the doors. My mouth is salivating. I'm ready to do my best to tackle one of those benches and accept whatever delicious meal has been prepared. I'm ready to feed this belly and clear up this hunger-laden confusion.

They're all behind those doors now and I can hardly wait. According to the restlessness around me, neither can my… peers? I'm not sure what else to call them.

The doors open, and out comes every single one of the people who were standing in front of us before, including Noland.

And they're all holding paper. Stacks upon stacks of paper reams. And buckets of paste.

Paper and paste.

Not food at all. No dino chicken nuggies.

CHAPTER SEVEN

Livvy

Stepping into this house, Mills's house, feels like visiting a ghost of a ghost. Everything smells like ash, wood, and memories. Only, I know in my heart of hearts Mills walked away, life and soul intact. There's no way she'd go down so easily. That girl is feisty and never held back from scrapping her way through whatever situation she found herself in.

"Looks like a skeleton, doesn't it?" Stark bites his lip while taking in the sight in front of us.

My brother is right. It does look like a skeleton, which is impressive. This house never felt like it stood on solid feet and yet, here she is, her bones and innards still upright. In fact, the entire entrance still exists. Yet, looking at her, she feels like she's been gutted. She was stronger than she looked, just like Mills.

"Mills called it her melting clock house. Seems pretty fitting now, doesn't it?"

"Yeah." He sucks in his breath before considering his next question. "You ready to go in?"

I shrug and look around us. No one else seems to be nearby. The entire excitement over a single arsoned house has dissolved in the last couple of days. It's as if all of Volga County has forgotten the incident happened at all, even though it has left a giant scar on Deuces Street. I guess everyone is too busy getting ready for exams or doing their frat party thing to pick at the scab that was growing in its place.

But not me.

I look at Stark, whose stone-hardened face says he's a scab-picker, too.

"Ready as I'll ever be," I finally answer him.

Carefully, we step over the police tape and onto the front porch, using our lightest touch to maneuver around the debris that leaked out. Everything holds surprisingly well. This is a good sign. The better intact the entrance to the house is, the better chance the rest of the house can be walked through, too.

Entering the house feels even more gutting than it did from outside. The kitchen is dark. Not from the lack of electricity. There's enough light creeping in through the windows to see the blackened walls and stained cabinets. From across the room, I can see the gaping hole where the door in the floor used to be. The little kitchen table is still there but blackened and tarred. Though I know better, I'm afraid if I were to touch it, it would crumble into dust.

The warped clock Mills always called her melting clock has fallen from its place and landed in a pile of dusty debris. I stare at that dead clock, wondering what time it was when it fell. "Think it's safe to go in further?"

Stark considers this for a minute, then clicks his tongue and whistles. "Liv, I'll go first, okay? I'll make sure it's safe. And even if you don't feel comfortable following me downstairs, it's okay. I don't blame you. You can stay up here, where at least there's some daylight. It might be safer that way."

Stark, the most caring big brother of all time. Somehow, I lucked out. Even if we did poke and pinch each other behind our parents' backs growing up, he never once backed down from standing guard or defense when I needed him to. This time is different, though. This time, it's for my friend, not me, and I don't need him to be the hero. Not alone, anyway.

I shake my head. "I'm coming with you, Stark. But sure, you go first. That way if there is a loose board somewhere you get the pleasure of breaking your neck before me." I stick my tongue out at him.

He sticks his out, too, and agrees, regardless of the fact that the stairs are actually concrete.

We shuffle through the burnt boards and cabinetry. Everything smells like an after fire, and it makes me glad I have some kind of sixth sense for knowing Mills got out. We get to the washing machine, and I marvel at the dark spot on its side, no doubt from where the fire peeked its head out of the floor and landed in the kitchen. Another ghostly memory fades in and out of me. Me and Mills, tearing apart that machine to fix the jam inside. Just as I recall us jumping up and down, the image goes up in smoke. Amazing that the fire department was able to kill it before it took down the entire house.

The door that hid the basement away is long gone, but the metal hinge is clearly bent open. Whoever was here last, this door was left open and in a hurry. Though, looking around me, it doesn't take much sleuthing to understand why. If the house was burning down around them, of course they weren't going to stop to put everything away where it belongs.

Stark takes a look down the hole to investigate. "All looks good. At least, from what I can tell from here." He pulls out his phone to use it as a flashlight. "I think we'll be okay, Liv. Be careful, though. Sometimes looks can be deceiving and what seems nice and sturdy could still crack from under you."

"Got it, Stark. Now, can we stop talking so much and just move?"

"You're the boss, sis."

Mimicking his movements, I also take out my phone and turn on the flashlight so I can watch each step as I take it. Together, we take precious steps all the way to the basement. The floor is exactly as it's always been. Cold. Concrete. Besides a little cracking and murky staining, there is no sign of aging or movement. It's the epitome of what everyone on the surface has been like. Completely stoic and stagnant. Unchanged from the local tragedy. But evidence of the aftermath is read all over the walls where flames once licked them clean with singe marks.

"Stark, look." I point out the gas stove with my phone light. What was once a dingy white is now blacked and tarred. It wears a permanent smoky halo. I close my eyes and think about what this means. My guess? This is where Mills last stood. "You see the burn marks around it? I bet that's where the fire started."

I look back up the stairs. The reports said arson. Which means one of two things: Either some crazy arsonist was hanging out with Mills in her basement, or Mills was pushed to the edge to set her own place on fire. Both scenarios mean she wasn't alone.

Everything inside me heats up as my blood heats to the boiling point. Whoever must have been standing right here with Mills is the reason for her being missing. And they're also the reason she almost died.

If only I could figure out who that is and get my hands around that slimy creature's neck and make them bring her back. Then again, I don't have to think too hard to figure it out. I have a strong feeling I know exactly who that person is.

"Look, Liv…" Stark's voice trails off, and I follow his finger. Mills's mural, or what's left of it. Most had burned away, but there are still traces of the painting she made. The map of Volga in abstract shapes and lines.

I can still remember the circles that indicated the murders Mills followed. She wanted so badly to figure out who was behind them, but even more, she wanted to share those girls' stories the only way she knew how. I was proud of her for using her talent for that.

Screw that. I *am* proud of her.

But then my eyes trace to where we're standing right now. And there's something that wasn't there before: a faint circle that mirrors all the others.

My heart feels a million times heavier. It's like all the iron in my blood has accumulated to the one spot in my chest, sinking every feeling that lives there. So, I was right. Everything was leading to her. Professor Elsinger's twisted drink laced with ricin to poison the girls, that look in his eye, the way he tackled me in the street. There is zero doubt in my mind. He was here. Everything was leading him to her.

"Stark, he has to have her."

"That professor?" So his train of thought led to the same place mine did.

I nod. "Professor Elsinger. I guarantee it. He hasn't been on campus since the day of the fire. All his classes have been canceled when his students have shown up without a professor. He was after her, Stark. He came after me when I was in the way of going after Mills. All of the reports have said no one was found inside. If he is still alive, he has her."

"So, where do you think they are?"

I shrug. "I wish I knew that answer."

We take a quiet walk around the basement, hoping the light on our phones doesn't fade out. Mills's art tables are nearly non-existent. All her supply drawers are charred on the surface. What must have been paint jars and brushes scatter the floor in unrecognizable blobs.

Her paintings. I can't believe I forgot her paintings. They were so important to her, I can't possibly imagine them disappearing into dust. "Stark!" I grab his arm. "Stark, Mills's paintings, we got them out, right?" The light on my phone juts over to his face, lighting it up to see his thoughtful expression.

"Right." He nods. "All the ones that were here, anyway."

"Right. But didn't she say she needed another one? One more to submit to the art gallery?"

He scratches his chin, and I can imagine the little stubbly hairs twitch under his finger. "Yeah, she did say that."

"Do you think she ever finished it?"

Even in the dark, I can see his dark brows knit together. "I don't know, Liv. Do you think she had the time?"

"Look, Mills may sit on deadlines until the last minute, but she was determined to have a complete collection. And when inspiration strikes her, no matter how crazy or morbid that inspiration is, she paints. And quickly. It's what she does, and she's damn good at it."

"So do you think inspiration struck her?"

My lip tastes like blood from biting it so hard. "I'm not sure we'll ever know the answer to that."

And those words force more weight in my chest than what was already there.

We continue our walk around the basement while my mind races. I can picture Mills sitting at one of these tables. I can almost see her with a paintbrush in hand. My eyes close and I try so hard to picture what she might have seen or felt or heard or anything. But my body freezes up. I don't have the gift of seeing things the way she does. I can't just feel it out and know what happened instinctually.

"Unless."

My eyes shoot open as Stark breaks my thoughts. They follow the light on his phone, shining off to the side.

"The alcove."

The words barely escape me. Mills had pointed out that the little alcove in her basement was like its own tiny bomb shelter with the ability to protect whatever was stashed inside. That's where she kept her finished painting before. And judging by the way Stark's hand is squeezing in there, he must believe that's where our friend stashed her final work of art.

"Liv, you'll never guess."

"There's a painting in there?" The weight in my heart lifts.

"There are two."

Now, I'm equally confused as I am excited. What was Mills up to? I rush over to help him ease out the canvases. They're singed at the corners, with a little black coating, but other than that, they're still intact. In great shape. This really was the protection she had hoped for.

I hold one painting up. It's beautiful. Large strokes of paint cover the entire thing. It's like a collage of colors. At first, I can't make it out. But when I hold it further away and we shine both of our lights on it from a distance, I can tell it's a girl, lying on the ground. She's got the same curly hair I do, a puff on top of her head. And her dark skin almost melts into the background. I feel sorry for her. And oddly enough, I feel an attachment to her, as if I've been in her shoes before.

"Stark, was there another girl? After Sam?"

He shakes his head and counts on his fingers. "Andrea, Malory, and Sam. Unless you count the girl that disappeared last Summer, that was it. After that, Mills disappeared."

A closer look at the details and it hits me. That curly hair on this girl's head? The street she's lying on? I had been in her shoes before. This is me. Mills painted me after Noland tried to add my body to his count. My heart explodes and melts and stitches itself back up. If Mills painted me, what must she think happened?

Carefully, I place the canvas down so we can focus on the second one. Stark holds it up and I aim my light. This one is black and white with the tiniest amount of blue. Another girl. This one with two braids. It's Mills, caged in, with a butterfly trapped with her.

My heart is in ribbons. Is this how Mills saw herself? Trapped? Needing to break free?

As much as I want to, I can't sit in this feeling too long because footsteps sound off above us. We aren't alone.

"Liv, hurry, hand it to me." Stark's panicked voice has me tripping over my own thoughts. I grab the canvas I put down and shove it in his direction.

As he scrambles to get both canvases together, two voices join in on the footsteps' melody.

"He said down there."

"Down those steps?"

"Yup."

"You got a light?"

A strong yellow beam clicks on by the top of the staircase.

I look to Stark. He looks at me. My feet feel glued to the floor and a part of me thinks that Mills would have had a joke about that. Something about leaving paste behind or purposefully keeping me here past my time or, I don't know. It's hard to think of a Mills quip when I have no idea who or what we're about to face.

Stark's hand hits my shoulder and I don't have time to consider any more about what Mills might have said.

The yellow light blinds both of us, and we're frozen from the shock.

"Who are you?" a man's voice asks, but I can't even see his face.

I consider telling him my full name, just blurting out, "Livvy Louise Landon," as if my life depends on it, because maybe it does. But my voice doesn't want to work.

"Who are you?" Stark echoes back, and I determine that my brother is way more confident at confronting men than I am. He can take this one.

The light shifts from our eyes to this man's face. His partner is standing next to him. They're both in all linen, from head to toe, with little hoods handing off the back of their heads.

"Do you have permission to be here?" the man asks us.

"The question is, do you have permission?" Stark answers a question with a question. I wish I had that kind of confidence.

The second man pulls out a paper from his hand. "According to this, we not only have permission, but we have orders by the owner to enter the property and collect a few requested items."

The first man jabs him. I'm guessing he didn't want his partner to mention any more than was necessary. Proof of their permission is probably enough.

"So unless you also have permission," the light shines in our faces again, "and I'm assuming you don't, then you are trespassing."

Stark gives the men a salute and grabs my arm. "We didn't know, sir. Just figured this building was abandoned after everything went down. We were just curious." He pushes me forward, leading me to the stairs.

The man with the paper folds it up and shoves it back into his pocket. "That's right, you move," he says. "Get on out before we call the authorities."

"Eye, eye captain," Stark mumbles, and the two of us carefully make our way back up, out into the open, and back into daylight.

When we reach the open, I throw Stark's hand off my arm. "What was that about?" I ask him.

He shakes his head. "I don't know who they were, but I didn't want to stay and find out. They looked pissed, and I didn't want them to get trigger-happy seeing us there. They didn't exactly seem like the friendly neighborhood people."

I swallow. Nod. They really didn't feel neighborly in the slightest. But then a new fear hits me. "Stark, where are Mills's paintings?"

He doesn't look me in the eye. "I put them back."

"You put them back?" I could scream at him for not being careful, but then he nods.

"I did. But you know what? That might be for the best."

I could strangle him. My brother, the man I looked up to my entire life, I could wrap my hands around his throat and choke the life out of him. I'm pretty sure my face relays that message. "What. Do. You. Mean?" Each word punctuates out of my mouth.

"You heard them, Liv. They were there to collect something. And I don't know about you, but the only thing I saw worth collecting were those paintings."

"So you're saying?"

"I'm saying that if they take those paintings out of the house, and if we can figure out where they go, we can find Mills."

CHAPTER EIGHT

Mills

"Thank you for choosing to be a part of our family. Please use the provided materials in front of you to create whatever you'd like. We're excited to watch your exploration of art take place."

The lady with fiery red hair and glasses is gone. So is Noland and all of his buddies. They all followed her out of the door, and I'm sitting here feeling completely out of place, with this recording playing through speakers in the room. Over. And. Over.

I'm feeling better now. Well, I guess the term "better" is relative. I'm better than the drugged feeling I had with the mask on my face. And I'm better than being blinded and led into a room that looks like it might give me food but gave me paper mâché instead. But overall? I'm not so sure how to take being in a room. Full of people. All who enthusiastically listened to some crazy lady in linen making speeches about how grateful we should be to be here. But, hey, at least I don't feel like I'm a cloudy mind forcing my body to move when it didn't want to.

I'd be better-better if I could get a good meal in my stomach. Or get a glass of water. Or if I felt like I could walk out of this place on my own free will, never to look back again. Ever. Unless it was to tie Noland up to an uncomfortable chair for hours while I starve him to death. That might make me feel better-better, too.

Or at least if I could understand his gig here. If I could get a grip on what his endgame is. But here I am, sitting on a bench seat with a long table in front of me. And all the other people who were sitting on the floor with me before are now sitting on the bench, too. There are ten of us together. Such a roundly specific number. And while I'm sitting in my place wishing for anything to fill my stomach with, all nine of these other people are adjusting themselves in their place. Some are even reaching into the boxes of paper that have been handed out to us.

I, too, pull a piece of paper out of the box in front of me. It's soft, as far as papers go. I can easily see through it, but at the same time, it feels sturdy. This is luxury paper. The kind specialty stores would stock for people who craft with expensive stationery.

"Pretty nice, isn't it?" a voice next to me asks.

I turn and see a young man with wispy blond hair dangling in his face. His face lights up by just opening his mouth, as if he's been waiting to have a conversation with anyone willing to sit down and listen.

"Yeah," I tell him, but it feels weird engaging in this conversation. Or any conversation, really. I don't know why. No one ever gave us a set of rules we have to follow. No one ever said, "Thou shall not speak with thy neighbor."

"Exciting, too, right?" He even nudges me, as if we're now sharing in the next thrilling event of our lives. A graduation. A new career. A party to welcome us out of retirement of whatever we left behind the doors to this place.

"Please use the materials in front of you—"

I try to ignore the recording seeping into my ears. It's clear he's trying to ignore it, too.

He gives a little fit of a giggle. "I already know what I'm going to do, do you?"

I look at the paper in my hand, already instinctually ripping it into pieces. What am I going to make? Who knows. This isn't my jam. Paint and canvas is where my heart is. But I guess if supplies and time are given, I'll let my hands explore the possibilities. The sign of a true artist is being able to create, no matter what, right?

Right, I convince myself.

"A lion," he says. And I almost forget that this guy is talking about his own project. "I'm going to make a lion."

I picture a handheld mounted lion's head. A prized possession of a wanna-be hunter displayed on a wall trying to fool someone of the strength and pride of the person who owns it. I look over at the spindly boy. His wire-frame tells me he'd never be caught dead in a jungle with a hunter's cap on.

"Don't you want to know why?" Clearly, this boy has to talk. As if he'll explode if the words don't come out.

I shrug. I don't really care to know why. I'd rather focus on my hands. Allow them to do their thing. As my fingers dance around strips of paper, I'm already seeing what might form in front of my eyes. Something strong itself. Long. Pointy. A weap—

"I was king."

Excuse me?

My eyes jut back over to this boy. Who, now that I see some prickles on his chin, he might not be as young as I thought. He might actually be a little older, in his mid-twenties even.

He shrugs back at me, and all of a sudden his voice turns down a tone. Even though his eyes are looking at mine, I can tell that's not where they're focused. Their aim is at something I can't see: a memory.

"That's what they called me in the mangliu, anyway."

Okay, now I need to know. "Mangliu?" I ask.

His eyes come back into focus for a split second. "She speaks! And here I was thinking she didn't want to draw any attention to herself because…" He vaguely gestures to my face.

My burns. I almost forgot about them. Compared to my rumbly tummy and my dry throat, the skin on my face feels completely normal. I guess whatever goo Noland slathered on my face has acted as some kind of miracle cream, healing it faster than it otherwise would have.

The blond next to me realizes his mistake, calling attention to what I really didn't need him to call attention to. He shakes his head, then addresses my question. "A blindly floating population." And when he sees I still don't understand what he's trying to tell me, he says, "A group of homeless boys." Just like that, his eyes go back to the memory he's recalling.

"They called me king because I was the one who could always track down food. Dumpster diving behind grocery stores. Scrapping through the back alley of restaurants. And once in a while, a fresh pizza whenever I worked the streets for money."

He must have felt my questioning eyes on him. "Nothing too shady. I didn't sell sex or anything. Not that I could find too many men I wanted to do that with anyway. And, well, I might be dumb enough to land myself without a roof over my head, but I'm not dumb enough to get naked in a back alley with a stranger. There are better ways to fill a stomach or two that have nothing to do with physical touch. I was pretty awesome talking to strangers. Just striking up conversation. And usually walked away with more money than anyone else in the mangliu just because people didn't want to see such a nice young man struggle any more than he was.

"Anyway," he continues, "I fed the pack. I was the king. The lion. It's what kept me surviving there. So if there's anything that represents moving forward and new adventures, it's a lion."

He gives me a toothy smile, as if he's memorized this speech. And I realize if he really was on the street for a while, then yeah, maybe he has been sitting on his victory story for a while.

"And you?" He nudges me again, even with his hands wrist deep into paste. He's clearly in a zone of create and chat.

As a kid, I was on the streets, too. Not in the same way. Actually, not anywhere close. Every night, I'd choose to leave the house and peruse the streets. I'd find what was going on and uncover the secrets everyone else was hiding.

I definitely saw more than I should have. And if this kid. Sorry, this guy, was living on the streets, not just visiting them, I imagine he probably saw more than he should have, too.

Maybe he did deserve to be king.

Or, at least a lion of some kind within a pack.

I don't give him an answer, though. I can't share a survival story like his. Especially when mine might still be going on.

"A hot air balloon," a girl beside me pipes up. Her chin-length hair flips into her face. Strawberry red strands curtain over her eyes.

My eyebrows raise at her.

"I know, I know. You didn't ask." Her hair still swings in her face, her gaze cast down on the work in front of her. Her hands collect wet strips of her own, and she's already working out how they fit together. "But I figured if you're going to talk to someone, you might as well talk to someone who will talk back."

Hey! I don't scoff out loud, but that feels like a dig at me when this chick doesn't know a thing about who I am or what I've been through up to this point.

My hands dip a few strips back into paste. I wonder if what they're making will actually work.

"It'll be tricky to do it round enough, but I figure if I bend them this way," I watch her shape these wet strips into a cuplike shape, holding the curvatures in their place so they don't flop over, "I think it'll work out."

"Were you a… balloonist?" the blond boy asks. And as silly as his question sounds, he's not joking. His face is as serious as when he told his own story.

Clearly, he's begging to hear hers.

She shakes her head. "No, but I've always liked the way hot air balloons easily rise. They escape. It's like magic, how easy it is you can climb in and just… go away. I can't tell you how many times I've wanted to do that. Especially after—"

She pauses, then looks up at the both of us. "I know, I know. Sad sappy story and all that. But you know, they were her favorite, too."

"I'm sorry, her?"

He really is digging, isn't he?

"My nana. I grew up with her. She's the one who raised me until she couldn't anymore. As crazy as she drove me, she was the one person who actually cared. She'd make me my favorite dinner and tuck me into bed, even when I was too old for it. Then the next day, she'd turn around and forget who I was. Those days, she'd throw silverware and plates at me and tell me to get out of her house. But all it took was a picture of a hot air balloon to bring her back to her normal self. She was old and senile, but she was my nana." At the realization of how much of her personal story she let spill, she sucked in a breath and hung her head even lower. "She always wanted to see a hot air balloon before she took her own life. Never did, though. So, I guess this is my way of doing it for her."

We're all quiet for a moment. The only sounds near us are the squelching of paste and the recording that's still feeding into our ears.

I don't want to ask her anymore about her nana. I've seen firsthand how that kind of thing can break a person. Well, maybe not first-first hand. But I've been close enough to notice its effect. Again, things I shouldn't have seen as a kid but did anyway. Things I don't want to think too much about in this moment, or any.

Then the guy beside me starts back up. "I'm Zak, by the way." Zak holds out a hand. It looks dry, cracked, and full of little spots that have glued itself together. Definitely an artist's hands I can appreciate. But I don't take it. I'm not sure I can trust the pearly white smile he's showing off.

I nod, instead. That should suit as enough of an answer for now.

"Fine." He shrugs. "I just figured that if we were going to be here together, we might as well get to know one another. It'd be nice to have a friendly face to talk to."

"Paula," the redhead next to me offers.

The two exchange glances across from me, a silent agreement of friendship.

Looking down at my hands, I see they've been hard at work. Crafting a cylindrical handle. All that's left is the blade at the end. "Mills," I cough up, deciding I want to be a part of this agreement, too.

"She speaks! She does have a name!" Zak laughs, and I have to admit his smile is charming.

Paula's cheeks flush and she giggles, too. I guess we're three peas in a pod, just crafting away at a table of goo. She goes back to fiddling with her own wet paper strips, turning them over each other to create a rounded shape. I'm mesmerized by the way she's able to do so without the aide of a balloon or ball or anything else.

Zak also returns to ripping his own paper into strips. "Looks like we're starting up our own little family, already huh?" His elbow nudges my shoulders in jest. Then under his breath, I think I hear him whisper, "Sister."

"A family away from the banals," Paula agrees. But her wording confuses me.

"The banals?" I ask. "As in…?"

"The borings," she answers. "People who don't know how to have fun with something like, well," she dips another strip in the paste and lifts it up to let it drip back into the bowl "with something like this." She gives a meek smile as she runs two fingers down the wet strip to clear off the excess.

"Exactly. It's kind of nice to be around people who get it." Zak mimics Paula's actions and he, too, is creating something roundish.

Absent-mindedly, I dip my papers in paste, too.

"It really is like being around a family," Paula agrees.

The recording echoes her thoughts, "Thank you for choosing our family."

And as the recording continues to tell me I'm here for artistic exploration, I explore the images floating in my mind and land on the reason for the object forming in my hands. The Machete Man.

To my right, Paula's crafting a hot air balloon. To my left, Zak is making a lion head. He gestures to what he's already finished, then nudges my arm to point at mine. "Hey, sister, you're not bad at this. But if you're really wanting to excel, you're going to have to do better than that."

Zak laughs. I can't tell if he's joking or serious.

"Better than what?" I ask.

"Better than a stick." His voice is deadpan. He is serious.

"It's not a stick." I'm confused. What does he mean? "It's a machete. A paper machete."

"Well, you'll have to do better than a paper machete to excel much further."

There's that word again. Excel. And I look at the creation in my hands. I thought it was good. But now I'm second-guessing. Is it good enough? Then again, I don't even know who or what it has to be good enough for.

Excelling, I guess.

CHAPTER NINE

Noland

Everything feels so easy right now. It's all playing right into my hands. I've got my Emily exactly where I need her and all that's left is to make sure she carries on just the way she is.

I left her a few minutes ago in the cafe with all the other recruits. Some of them seem like they've got plenty of potential. Excitement, too. They seem so ready to take on the task of doing something so easy and fun: paper mâché. I'm sure it's been years since some of them have even touched a bowl of paste like that. I can't wait to see how the re-introduction sparks their imaginations.

I wonder what Mills will make. Some kind of hybrid animal in motion? An abstract piece that's uniquely her own? Or maybe she'll blow us all away with a lifesize sculpture of something fantastic, like Michelangelo's David.

Honestly, it doesn't matter what she comes up with. Our names are already a shoo-in. This exercise is just to get her — them — acquainted with Memento Mori. Make them feel welcome into the family we're building. Give them something to do with their hands while their minds are soaking in the truth about who we all are. Because our truths are important. Our truths are going to save those who deserve it from this banal realm we call "reality."

It's not the real reality. It's just what we're conditioned to believe. There's something so much better waiting for us on the other side.

While all the recruits are diligently working, their handlers are learning. If we are to be part of The Circle, then we have to know our truths, as well. We move from the first floor, which is where recruits are temporarily housed. A few rooms to accommodate our needs. We are the recruits' support network, after all. And you can't hold a support network hostage from those who need it. That's what the "reality realm" does. Here, we know the dangers of that.

Every step I take away from the first floor feels like success. It's like I'm taking another step into my fate. I'm so ready for it. Just a few more strides up, and I'll reach the second floor. The floor waiting for me.

I open the door from the corridor and am welcomed by smiling faces. Each one has proven themselves to be worthy enough to be here. At least temporarily. We shall see once we're judged at the gallery.

Until then...

"Noland, welcome!" The Dignitary welcomes me. "Come in, come in. We have something special today."

I nod my recognition to her, but I know my place. I know I shouldn't speak to her yet. Not directly, anyway. Not here in front of everyone. The rules state not to speak to her unless she approaches you first and invites you to a conversation. So, I keep my mouth shut and walk inside the classroom.

There are ten seats. One for each handler. Mine is the only open one left, right smack dab in the middle of the room. I take my seat, sliding in like it was built just for me.

"Thank you for coming today," says The Dignitary, as if we had a choice. Of course we were going to come. We've all made the promise from day one. We're devoted to being better, doing better, becoming better. And if The Dignitary says to meet on the second floor for a special announcement, we will be there. "Today, I have a special lesson planned."

Every single one of the handlers adjusts his or her self in their seats. I lean forward. I want to take in everything she says.

"Good afternoon, Mori handlers!"

"Good afternoon," we all chime back in perfect unison, but I feel my voice is stronger than the others. I hope she can hear it above the rest. Every bit of positive impression will help me in the long run.

"As you know," she starts back up, "we are in the process of creating The Circle, the group of carefully selected artists who are approved to go to the next realm with special privilege. Final approvals will be made on March 15th, thanks to the Volga community and their gracious acceptance of our offer to sponsor this year's fine arts gallery and auction."

Chills run down my spine, and they must run through the entire room because everyone adjusts in their seats again. Some are smugly smiling, sure they'll be sitting next to me when we're gifted the seats in The Circle. Others nervously twitching, not so certain they'll be accepted.

"But this is all information you already know." The Dignitary fiddles with her glasses for a moment to make a point. "Today, I'm bringing you new information. Information that will explain what you need to know as potential Circle members."

Everyone's eyes are attentive now. Everyone is adjusting their stance to hear better. Because everyone wants in on the information that may give them a competitive edge.

"I have been keeping myself in meditation a few hours every day for the past few days, with the attempt to speak with Dali da Monet, and listening to what She has to say."

Dali da Monet, the collective voice of our artistic ancestors. The ones who guide us all on our journeys and who informs The Dignitary of where each of us falls on the master plan of our lives. She only speaks to The Dignitary and only in a meditative state. That's why she always locks herself in the only room on the top floor. No one else is allowed up there. Not even security. The only person she sometimes allows in is Doctor James to give her vitality through vitamins and elixirs. Even then, it's on a strict schedule. Once a month on a Wednesday morning.

And even then, he needs to provide three forms of identification before he uses his keycard to get in.

"And I sat in the quiet for fifteen hours straight, waiting for Her to speak first. My patience brings you gifts, friends. Dali da Monet has finally told me the message we, as artists, are to provide for the world."

The room erupts with applause. A few people whoot. One woman with long black hair breaks into tears. We've been waiting for this for a long time. Since initiation into the society. We always knew there was a message we were supposed to deliver to the world, a message that would deliver us into the next realm, the realm after banal reality. But we never knew what the message was that we were supposed to deliver.

"I think it's time we do an experiment. Something that's never been done before, but as open to communication as Dali da Monet was, I think She's ready. She's ready to speak to you all."

As much as I'd think the room would have erupted again, it didn't. Everyone is stone still. Shocked. We're all statues without bones and plastered smiles on our faces. Could it be true? Could the Dali da Monet actually want to speak with us? With the handlers who have yet to be selected for The Circle or not? This is unheard of, and yet, The Dignitary is right here, standing in front of this classroom with an eager look on her face. She seems to think it's true.

And if she believes it to be true, then it must be.

"Everyone, please close your eyes."

I close mine. Dark curtains engulf me. All I see are the imprints of light splotches against my eyelids. But soon, after a moment or two, those vanish, too. I welcome the blackness. Because the blackness is where I can hear the collective voices if they're ready to speak to me. If she is ready to speak to me.

"Now, I need you to be in a relaxed state. Lean back in your seats. Get out of them if you need to. Climb onto the floor and lay down.

Stretch out. Get as comfortable as you can. Dali da Monet will only come to you if your body — your vessel — is prepared for Her."

I slide back into my seat, pretending my body is completely boneless. But I still feel rigid. So I slide out of the seat and feel the cold floor under me. My body relaxes on it, feeling every corner of the tiles and where they meet up with one another. My muscles melt away as much as my bones do and all I'm left with is skin and bloody innards. I breathe in and out in a steady motion, purposefully moving my lungs, willing them to expand and retract, as I imagine the blood in my body whooshing around to all the places it's supposed to go.

"Now, breathe in deeply," says The Dignitary. "When you don't feel like you can hold any more air into your lungs, keep sucking it in. Then, let it out. With control. Don't let it escape until you've allowed it to. Each breath in and each breath out is a welcoming message. You're telling Dali da Monet that you're ready for Her. You're opening up the doors to your soul for Her."

I focus on The Dignitary's voice. With intention, I do breathe in. And even when my lungs feel like they're going to burst, I suck in more air, filling them up to complete expansion. And when she says, "Breathe out," I exhale. Slowly. I don't even count. I just feel the burn within me and will myself to exhale through it.

I don't care if it hurts. It doesn't matter. No pain matters because as long as Dali da Monet is coming, I'll be free of it all. She will take it away, and I will feel light, airy, ready for whatever is next. She will take the hurt and the pain and turn it into nothingness. Even the pain of watching my Mills, my recruit, and not being able to have her. It won't matter. Nothing will matter.

The Dignitary tells us to breathe in again, so I do. The process repeats itself over and over. "Breathe out," she says again, and I allow the air to disperse around me in a controlled time. This pattern repeats again. Minutes go by. An hour. And I'm still waiting patiently. I want to hear what the collective voices say, what our artistic ancestors have in store for me. Because if They don't have the answer to my life's purpose, then nobody does. So I wait. Patiently.

The room is quiet. Everyone else is waiting patiently, too.

The breathing in the room has turned into a singular movement. Everyone is sucking in the same air at once, fighting over the same molecules, collecting what they can for themselves. And then, everyone blows it all out at the same time, too. The carbon dioxide fills the space around us until it's unbreathable, and then it shifts again to consumable CO_2.

We're all waiting. We're all wanting.

Then, all of a sudden, I hear a gasp. It's light. Barely audible, but it's there. I dare not open my eyes. I dare not see who made the noise or ask what is happening because if this really is Dali da Monet, then I need to pay attention. I need to ask myself for more patience. I need to keep on doing the breathwork, even if it takes me another hour to do.

Another gasp. This one must be from another person because it sounds slightly different. Deeper, even. I can almost hear the voice behind it, and I bet it's Jon.

I breathe again. In. Out. Deeper. Longer. Stronger.

Why isn't Dali da Monet talking to me? Why can't I hear Her voice?

Mentally, I take a step back. Because if The Dignitary says she waited fifteen hours, then I can wait it out for at least that much. Maybe more. I don't care that others are experiencing something I haven't yet experienced.

Except, I do care. A lot.

I just don't want to be left out. I don't want to lose out on the possibility of hearing the utmost important voice I could ever experience in my lifetime.

And that's when it happens. I feel a shiver, tiny little prickles, that start on my forehead and tiptoe their way down my spine, my arms, and all the way to the tips of my toes. My entire body feels lifted, higher.

I don't hear any voices, but I feel Them, the entire collective. They're in me, around me, through me, and they're telling me how important I am.

I do hold importance. I am here for a reason, and it's a great thing that I've brought the recruit I did because I am fulfilling my prophecy as well as the Society's.

And as soon as I feel the tingling sensation in every fiber of my being, it's gone.

I was lifted into the air, and now I'm on the floor. I feel the cold tile. I feel the divots between them. I'm back in the room, with everyone else around me and The Dignitary watching us from the front.

I open my eyes. Everyone else is awake. Eyes peeled wide. And The Dignitary is smiling, even through her thick eyeglasses.

"Did you feel it?" she asks, and I nod. I did. I felt everything, and judging by the silence in the room, I'm assuming everyone else did, too.

Dali da Monet did speak to us. And Her voice comes in prickles and pins, staticy moments that leave us dizzy.

"I knew you would," The Dignitary says. She turns her back to us and auditorily takes one more deep breath. I can hear the air actually enter her lungs as she lifts her palms up to the ceiling.

"Dali da Monet, thank you!" she bellows out into the open.

I feel pinpricks again. The slightest movement has my extremities waking up from their sleep state. But again, it's Dali da Monet. She is still speaking to me, even as my body wakes up from my moment with Her and drifts back into this realm of reality. She is still here. With me. In me. Guiding me.

Guiding me to stand.

Guiding everyone else to also stand.

And before I know it, we are all on our feet, facing The Dignitary and mimicking her movements. My palms raise up to the ceiling as well, mirroring hers.

"Thank you for your words!" she bellows out again, and instinctively, the entire room echoes, "Thank you!"

We all stand like this, welcoming the messages from Dali da Monet for as long as we're supposed to, as long as we're instructed to.

Then, the moment passes and The Dignitary turns around to face us again.

"Sit," she instructs.

So we sit. We wait. We listen.

"Today is a very special day. Never before has Dali da Monet ever spoken to a group. Keep in mind, this may not happen again. But I knew She was ready. And now, you have all felt her presence."

She walks down one aisle. "Now, I know you may be confused. You're probably trying to decipher what you felt from the collective. You haven't yet learned how to understand Her language. So confusion is understood."

She walks up another aisle. "So allow me the pleasure to translate." When she reaches the front of the room, she stares at us through her thick, all-knowing glasses. "Ladies and gentlemen. We are the message for the world."

All eyes stare back at her, begging for an elaboration.

"Did you hear me?" she yells out. "WE are the message. It's us! You! I! All the artistic ancestors who have come before us! It's our collective voices, all of us. It's our identity! Our craft! Our souls! All of us!"

Then, she lowers her voice and in barely a whisper, repeats, "It's us, friends. We are the message to the world. We are the keys to ourselves. And I don't know about you, but that is the most amazing news I have heard in a very, very long time."

Satisfied with her speech, The Dignitary claps her hands together and links her fingers. We're all stunned into silence, unsure of what our next move should be. "Thank you so much for being a part of this special experience today. You have all earned it. But for now, I need you to gather your things, including your recruits, and prepare. Only two more days and the real judgment begins."

The sounds of metal chair legs scraping against the tile fills my ears as The Dignitary's words dig into my memory.

The message the world needs to hear is us. It's all of us.

"Noland Elsigner," she approaches me, and I realize I'm the only one left sitting. This isn't a generic greeting everyone gets. As the only two people here, this is an invitation to speak. So I do. I say the only thing that makes sense to me.

"Apologies, Dignitary." I fumble my way to a stand, brushing the legs of my pants. "Apologies." I hang my head.

"Noland Elsigner, there is no need to apologize." I look up to see her smiling. "In fact, I'm glad you stayed behind. I have something extra special for you."

More than the experience I just had? Feeling the language of the artistic collective?

She reaches behind her and pulls out something from her pocket. "Here. For you."

She's beaming. Light nearly expands out of her teeth and enters my heart. In her hand is an envelope. Gingerly, I take it with the same care as a priceless artifact. In one palm, I lay it out. The other runs over the waxy seal with two Ms overlaid on each other.

An appreciation letter, from The Dignitary herself.

"Thank you," I gasp out. "Thank you!"

I move to rip the seal off, but she stops me. Her wrinkled hand touches mine. I can feel the gentle crevices in her skin. "Wait," she says. "Wait to open it until later. It'll mean more then. Promise. Just keep in mind, when you follow the rules, good things happen." Her hand moves off mine. "Now, go get your recruit, Noland. You'll both want to rest up."

So I do. My feet nearly float down the hallway, through the stairway, and all the way back to the cafe where I find all the recruits diligently working on their paper mâché projects. Mills is a beacon for me. I find her at the table with something long and pointed in her hands. A machete. A paper mâché machete.

Well, that's interesting.

I link my hand into hers and feel her pause. "Come," I say. "It's time to leave."

Back goes on her mask. And back goes my arm around her waist. I guide her back to our room where we are to sit and wait until the next phase.

I prop her onto the bed, where her breathing relaxes, and I make sure to poke her awake every time she gets closer to sleep. She needs to be awake, so she can wake up to the truth of Memento Mori.

While I wait for her drowsiness to dissipate for the night, I pull out the letter.

The Dignitary's words fill me up. My brain, my heart, my soul. If ever I needed proof of the power and love of the Memento Mori Society, this is it. Right here.

CHAPTER TEN

Mills

Dear: Mr. Elsinger

Please allow this letter to serve as an appreciation for your role in the Memento Mori Society. We have worked diligently to create and preserve the highest level of artistic genius within the walls of our confines.

Your knowledge and creativity have proven to be invaluable assets to our organization's values. Not only do we appreciate in the sharing of your experiences in education, but we are in constant awe of your diligence to keep our values front and center in everything you do. From where we stand, it appears that every choice you have made up to this point as well as every choice you continue to make, has been made with Memento Mori in mind. We appreciate your due diligence in doing so.

Not only have you brought us an incredible recruit for judgment, but you have also risked yourself and your reputation on the outside world to ensure her presence under our roof. Wherever your partnership with her may fall after judgment, she will be an asset to us just as you have been. For this, we thank you and your persistence.

We also want to extend our appreciation to you for keeping your bodily restraint in place. We understand that under our roof, it is difficult for the male handler to repress the natural urges which do not have a place here. You have proven that you are the embodiment of the MMS pillars we hold so close: Creativity, perseverance, and devotion.

Dali da Monet willing, you will pass the round of judgment and earn your place as a part of The Circle. You definitely hold an advantage.

We shall see you tomorrow. May the odds be in your and your recruit's favor. We look forward to what you have to offer our future.

Iris Mori
MMS Dignitary

Unbelievable. *Unbelievable*!

I must have dozed off a little, though I get the feeling I wasn't supposed to. All night long, Noland kept shaking me awake every time my eyes started to close. But at some point, he gave up his watch over me, and apparently over himself, too.

Just a few minutes ago, I woke up to see Noland on the floor, his back resting against the bed. I guess whatever rule that said he was supposed to keep shaking me awake expired. Grateful. I was so grateful to be allowed a little bit of rest. And then I woke up to this *delightful* letter on the floor next to him.

Now, with shaking hands, I cannot stomach the words of this letter. What does this even mean? He's admirable? Diligent? And about what? Forcing me here as his *recruit*? According to this letter, they're praising Noland for forcing me against my will to come here, to the 'confines of these walls.' How's that for admirable?

Oh and congratulations, Noland, for not forcing yourself on me in the worst perverse way anyone can think of. You're such a hero for not raping your precious recruit.

This is bullshit. And had I not seen it with my own two eyes, I would have never thought someone would literally write out a personalized appreciation letter for kidnapping and holding bodily restraint.

Not even in this hellhole.

Then again, he did let me rest. Which helped my stomach forget about food and drink for a little bit.

Careful not to wake him, I ease myself out of the covers and land a foot on the floor. It's cold, but I hold back any shiver. My other foot joins in on the shivery fun and I raise my weight on my toes. Maybe I can tiptoe myself out of here. If I could just sneak past him, I could open the door and find my way out.

Which is what I want, right? Out of the place that wants me to become part of their family?

I balance my weight on both of my big toes and take a step forward. So far so good. Noland isn't stirring. Carefully, I take another step. Good. Still no movement from him. I can do this. I will do this. The door to freedom is only a few feet away. I could probably lunge forward and grasp the doorknob in a single movement. But if I move too quickly, I'm sure Noland will get up, tackle me, and who knows if he'll have any self-restraint fighting me back. A third step and I can no longer see his face. It's behind me. So I turn around to check. Yes; still asleep.

I breathe a sigh of relief, and just when I feel like I'm home free, a sound erupts from outside the window. A freaking chainsaw. Of course someone would have to rev up a chainsaw first thing in the morning. I glare out the window. I need to see who is interrupting my sneaky escape.

Then again, a part of me wants it to wake him up. Then I can ask him about the letter. Maybe it's not what it seems. Maybe Noland has an explanation that makes sense. Maybe there's some explanation that can justify this entire situation, iron out all the crazy wrinkles and make it make sense.

The sound comes from one of the groundskeepers. He's wearing the standard linen garb everyone else is wearing. Well, everyone else except for recruits, and I'm beginning to wonder where the line is drawn between us and them. And when will I get to strip myself of the same clothes I've been wearing for a few days and finally wear something a little cleaner? And if I'm being honest, something that looks a lot more comfortable, too.

This man out the window isn't doing me any favors by making so much noise as he tears down the pine tree. I glance down at Noland, who must sleep as hard as he is determined. The chainsaw doesn't bother him at all. Carefully, I pivot and face the door again. Just a few more tiptoes and I'll be out that door. I can already see it now, running down a corridor, past all these confused, smiling faces, singing "adios" to all the people who forced us all here. I'd grab Paula and Zak, too, if I could. And we'd compare stories about being weirdos together. We'd swing the front doors open, breathe in the fresh air, and celebrate by running, running, running, as fast as we could away from this place and somewhere much, much better for us.

Except, were Paula and Zak forced here against their will? They didn't seem to be. They seemed to be pretty thrilled to be here. Just to have a place where they could do arts and crafts and be accepted. Not that I blame them. Their stories hit a little close to home for me, too. I get it. Seeing things you shouldn't at a time you never should. It would be easy to feel so lost, and so easy to feel so found in a place like this. A found family place. It does sound nice on the surface.

But not nice enough to not leave, right?

Another step and my stomach can no longer hold in its complaints. It growls like a grisly who has been locked up for far too long. I cross my arms, mentally telling it to stop. I beg the bear to be still for a moment. It's not so bad being there for right now. And then I promise it I'll feed it the moment I'm out. I'll feed it everything I can get my hands on. Mac and cheese. Dino nuggies. Pizza with the works. Chocolate pudding and three tall glasses of iced tea. I'll even get the biggest salad with all of the fancy greens I could possible get a hold of.

The bear in my stomach can't take it anymore. It's aggressively loud and demanding, and I cannot hold it back.

Noland stirs. He adjusts his position while I pivot on my toes again and take another step. Then two. Then three. I'm right at the door, and my hand is on the doorknob, ready to turn it and allow myself out, out, out into the open freedom!

But is it really freedom if I'm not with my people? The people who are like-minded and just as damn savvy as I am with a paintbrush and paint? Or, you know, at least paste and paper?

And Noland's hand is on my ankle. It's wrapped around it in a firm grip, reminding me that I'm here under his grasp, not my own.

Or maybe not entirely.

"Well, good morning, Sunshine." He winks at me.

I swallow back the sugar-coated venom I want to spew out at him.

"You weren't thinking about leaving me, were you?"

I look at my hand on the knob. I wasn't just thinking about leaving him. I was willing it to happen. I was begging for my reality to match up with my desires and I'd run ever so free. At least to Zak and Paula. I wanted to know their stories. I wanted to see what they saw. I wanted to feel what they feel. Maybe they'd let me paint their portraits, too.

I look back at him. His smirk hasn't adjusted an inch.

"You know if you were to end up on the other side of the door, they'd just bring you back to me, right?" He lifts himself off the floor. "There's nothing outside of these walls for you. You do have something special, and we can see that here. What you have is special enough to keep under our roof. In fact, go ahead." He gives me another one of his sickening winks. "Open the door. See what's on the other side waiting for you. Guarantee if you walk out, you'll find yourself right back here. The banal world outside of this place will kill you, Mills. It will suck you of your creativity and leave you high and dry."

I turn the knob, testing whatever is on the other side.

He responds with a shrug. "Don't tell me you've never felt that way, Emily. How many times were you in my office? Asking for some advice on how to make art worthwhile? All those people, all those voices, they've told you that art is a silly thing. It's a hobby that doesn't go anywhere past filling up your time. But you knew better, Mills, didn't you?"

My hand pauses on the knob. He's right.

"I knew it from day one, Mills. Before I ever saw your face. Before your name ever ended up on my roster. When you applied to Volga University, I knew you were meant for more. You talked about how you saw the beauty in life and in death and the relationship between it all. You knew there was something more to this life. You just didn't know that you'd need to get to the next realm to see it. You believed in your own talent, and I believed in you for it."

How many times had I found myself in his office almost in tears after someone tore down my creative dreams? How many times did I try to explain the importance of artistic expression to be laughed at as some pretentious creator? And how many times did he point out one of the classics and tell the stories about how they've changed society? How the Mona Lisa influenced direct metaphors in music and movies, how Andy Warhol commented on emotional flatness with his Marilyn Diptych, how The Birth of Venus is a multigenerational symbol of hope.

How many times did he assure me that what I was doing was important, regardless of what the rest of the world said? If it was important to me, it would be important to the world. In life, death, and the entire spectrum of it all in between.

How many times did he offer a warming touch? Not just in his office, but here. After my cleanse. So that I'd feel safe, secure, and like I'm exactly where I'm supposed to be?

"I always knew you had potential, Mills. You could be one of the greats, if you allowed yourself to be. You have the knowledge. You have the talent." He licks his lips at the last word. "You just need a place with people who can help you believe in yourself as much as I believe in you."

I drop my hand to my side. He's right. Absolutely right. He has protected me, and once a canvas was in the public eye, people would scoff and shudder. I was kicked out of college for it, for goodness sake.

The only time I felt like I was doing the right thing was when I was painting for the gallery. For *this* gallery. The one I've been pulled aside and pulled out of the "banal world" to attend.

I shake my head. Nope. Nope. Nope. I can't let these cluttered thoughts drag me into a corner of this hellhole where I'll never get out. My hand juts back onto the doorknob and I turn it.

"Noland, you're sick and twisted. Maybe you can trick some other fool into thinking your shit don't stink, but I'm not that kid." I don't want to believe I'm that kid. But the serene look on his face is a jut back into the days when I came to him crying and he eased every concern I ever had of not getting the right hue, the right position, or the right subject.

I yank the door open, ready to run. Ready to burst around the corner, knocking over anyone in my quest to find an escape. But I don't even get a chance to step a foot outside this room because there are two men standing there to greet me. One, is a man in a name tag without a name. The other is a man in a white coat. They both greet me in a smile and the body language of a barricade.

They each take a step forward, pushing me further back. Back into my place, where Noland insists I belong. Where, maybe I do belong. My feet step back, and I nearly trip over Noland's socked feet. He steadies me with two hands on my shoulders and I have to wonder, how the heck did he move so quickly to his feet?

The man in the white coat sandwiches me between himself and Noland. He looks me up and down, tilting his chin in a way that makes me believe he's scrutinizing my pores. Heat rises in my chest and the beast inside feels even more trapped than before. Not only is it in a cage without food, it's being gawked at by paying visitors.

"It really is doing the trick," he tells Noland, not me. Even though his eyes are on my face.

Noland's hands grip my shoulders, and the beast inside me feels chained down into submission. It's given up. Understanding that my face really is healing, and Noland has something to do with it. "She looks great, doesn't she?"

The man in front of me nods and reaches into his white coat. That's when I realize, this must be the doctor Noland's mentioned before. This must be the man who has helped him heal from whatever minor burns I gave him. With the way he's scrutinizing my facial features, I realize this doctor has also had his say into my own skin.

The goo Noland painted into my mask.

The stuff that stinks like pine.

The gunk that put me into a sleepy stupor.

Has probably also healed my burns.

He's healed me. Noland has healed me. Every muscle in my body turns into jelly as the realization washes through me. Noland has been helping me. He's been healing me. And he brought me here because of his belief in my talent.

The doctor pulls out a little jar from his pocket and hands it to Noland. They exchange knowing glances. A piece of the beast still wants to fight and break out of this cage. But a much larger piece knows whatever pine-scented goo inside that jar is doing me good.

And if that's good for me, maybe there's more good waiting in this place.

The other man standing behind the white-coat man reaches into his pocket, too. Only, he ignores Noland's presence entirely. He even pushes aside the other man to get to me directly. He stretches his arm out. Inside his palm is an envelope. One that matches the stationary Noland's note was written on.

I have my own love note. My own proof that the good in this place is not only waiting for me, it sees me, too. It's ready for me. And I think I'm ready for it.

CHAPTER ELEVEN

Livvy

"Stark." He doesn't even peek up from whatever catches his eyes' attention. Clearly, he's blocked out my voice yet again with his proverbial sister earmuffs on.

"Stark!" His eyes are still glued down, and his ears are still tuned out. There's nothing tearing him away from whatever the heck he has. It might as well be a gorgeous girl with alluring eyes and natural, bouncy… curls.

"Stark!" The noise my hand makes as it slams down on the countertop is just as loud as my yell. The *whack* finally jumps into consciousness.

"Oh, Liv, I'm glad you're here."

Much better. "You called me here, dummy."

He smiles at me, the way that says he's got something up his sleeve and can't wait to share it.

"So, why?"

"Why what?" he asks, but that look is still on his face. He knows something.

"Why did you call me between classes to meet you at work when you could have told me whatever it was over the phone?"

That's when he bites his lip and pushes forward the thing that was holding his attention before. A paper. A very detailed paper printed off with a Volga County seal.

"What's this?" I ask, even though there is a clear marking at the top of the page. It's a deed. A house deed.

"This is the deed to Mills's house." He slaps his finger down on the paper to point out the address on Forty-Second Street. The last time I saw the address in writing was when Mills was signing the renter's agreement. It hits me. His focus really was on a gorgeous girl.

I scan over the document, and it all floods back to me. All the little details, the fine print, and the signatures scrawled on all the papers. Only this one didn't hold Mills's name. Renters aren't owners. But when she signed on the dotted line of the renter's agreement, the same name was scribbled down on those papers as it is on here. The mention of it was so quick in passing my brain didn't register then. But it does now.

Noland Elsinger is the owner of the house.

"Sis, that's the professor's name, isn't it?"

I nod. "So if he's the owner of the house,"

"And those men had permission to collect whatever they found inside."

"Then he is definitely still alive. And, Stark," I look at him seriously while my insides twist up, "he knows where Mills is. He definitely has her. I know I thought it before, but this…" I tap my finger on the deed. "This is good enough to be proof."

He wiggles his eyebrows at me. "That's exactly what I thought, too."

"Stark, that man has not been on campus since the day of the fire. Last I saw him, he was running scared after poisoning girls several girls. You saw it yourself. There were two paintings that were left inside the basement. That man was insane when it came to art. He's not just after her, Stark. He's after her art. The question is why?" But I'm not sure the answer to that question even matters. What matters is that we find her and get her away from that creep. Then do whatever it takes to stop him from doing it again to anyone else.

He picks up the deed and looks it over with a frown. "I guess that's something we'd have to ask him."

"Well, it's not like we can find him with a forwarding address or anything, can we?"

He nods. "I think we can."

Of course he's thinking one step ahead of me. A second paper appears in his hands from behind the counter. He places that next to the deed.

This one is hand written and with a post office approval. Apparently, while I've been busy with classes, Stark's been busy clue-chasing around town. And this is a big one. Noland Elsinger's signature is on it. And scribbled next to it is an address. Only, the number in the address doesn't make sense.

000 Blackwell Ave.

"Blackwell Avenue. Isn't that where the big iron gate is outside town?"

Blackwell is one of those places you read about in the scariest of children's books. It's like where Hansel and Grettle's witch lives or where the Big Bad Wolf might hide out. Who knows. No one has ever really seen what might be behind the iron gate, but that's never stopped town lore from spreading about the place.

The story goes, whoever enters the property disappears behind the line of pine trees and out of sight forever. People go in, but they don't come out. The Big Bad Wolf eats them up whole.

I don't believe in children's stories, though. After all, if those men stepped foot into the Melting Clock House, it can't be true. Can it? They came from somewhere, and 000 Blackwell Avenue seems like just as good of a place as any to hold strange men in linen suits.

"Yeah," he says. "It's a short drive away. Most people stop to shake the gate and run off before anyone answers. They're too scared something is going to jump up and get them. But if that's where Noland's forwarding address is, then we've got to check it out. Think you're brave enough to stick around and see what's behind it?"

I ignore his jab at my nerves. "Why would he have a forwarding address in the middle of nowhere?"

And with such an odd number. Do people really have a zero house number?

Just then, someone clears their throat. Not me. Not Stark. Someone else who is standing over our shoulders and waiting to be acknowledged.

"Sorry, ma'am," Stark addresses her and swipes the papers away from sight. No need to invite a stranger's opinion on our research. Then, he ushers me off to the side with a look. He wants to address this woman's needs and get her on her way so we can get back to our work together.

I step away, making room for the lady in thick glasses and red hair. Her eyes are clouded by her thick prescription, but I can still see her angry wrinkles that live above her nose and between her brows. "Don't you think the two of you should take your conversation somewhere else? Somewhere where you're *not* going to get in the way of people trying to check out?"

Whoever this woman is, she clearly isn't happy with us or our nonsense in holding a conversation like two normal people do. I can feel all the cells on my skin dry up and crawl over my body.

"I'm so sorry, ma'am. Is this all for you?" Stark holds up a plastic sealed pouch labeled 'clay tools'.

Inside the plastic blisterpack are several tools with bamboo handles, each one with a different textured tip. I wonder what Mills would make out of such a thing. Or if she could even do something on canvas with these. Though, I guess not all artists are painters and some like to use materials I never saw Mills dabble in.

"Does it look like this is all?"

She steps aside to reveal a shopping cart she was somehow hiding behind her. It's filled with piles of more blister packs. Some are identical to the one Stark holds while others have miniature versions. There are a few that look like cheese graters and some that look like roughly textured mallets. Clay tools. That's what they've got to be. I can't imagine what else they'd be used for. And I can't imagine why a single person would empty a shelf of tools just for herself.

"Well, no, ma'am, I guess it doesn't."

My brother is a politeness saint. All I can think about is what Mills would say about a tiny redhead pushing around her weight in rudeness. I try to give this woman a polite greeting, too, but I don't think I'm built for addressing her with a smile.

"That's right; it's not all. Now, make sure you scan each and every one of them. And when you're done, check to see if there are more in the back."

More? I can only imagine the kind of joke Mills would crack at this. Something about building a shrine with them and worshiping art supplies? I don't know. I'm not nearly as quick as Mills is with her quips. That's always been her job.

"Yes, ma'am. I'll check the system right now." Stark punches a few buttons on the computer in front of him and bites his lip as he scrolls through the listings. "There are three more in the back I can ring you up for. Would you like for me to do that?"

The look in her eyes says he's making her dreams come true. Now she can really build up that shrine.

"Of course I would. Didn't I tell you I wanted you to? Or were you not listening?"

I think I see saliva make its way out of her mouth and onto the countertop in little droplets.

"Of course, ma'am. I'll ring you up right here for what's left. Then, I can go into the supply room and get the rest out for you. I'll help you carry them to your car, too, okay?"

Seriously, this man is too kind. No wonder all the girls make googly eyes at him with slack jaws and pointed fingers. There aren't too many kind and polite men in the wonderful world of Volga County anymore.

And I swear, there aren't too many girls around here who deserve what's left, either. So when I get a hold of Mills and bring her back, you better bet I'll be pushing for them to get together even harder than before. She deserves to be happy, and he deserves someone who will appreciate how happy he can make her. I just better not hear about whatever happiness they share behind closed doors. Gross.

The red headed woman eyes him suspiciously as she hands over a credit card. He swipes, hands it back, and makes his way to the back of the store.

Now, I'm left with this woman in front of me, eyeing *me* suspiciously. And I'm not sure why, but it makes me feel guilty for taking up this space, like I don't belong to simply stand here in front of her. I feel judged and put on display, so I try to think of anything else to bide the time until I can get back to my conversation with Stark. All I can come up with is: 000 Blackwell Avenue.

The three zeros spin in my head in little loops, little Os trying to give me oxygen.

"All the supplies you could possibly ask for all around you and you've got nothing in your hands?" She sucks in her words like she's smoking them.

"I guess we all can't be artistic geniuses, can we?" My words slip out like oil before I can dam them up with my nerves.

A nod, a smile, and a hand finds her hip. "You've got that right. Quite frankly, it's a breath of fresh air to hear you say that. Not everyone has a talent for it and too many people feel like they can slap a few things together with glue and paint and call themselves brilliant."

A half smile is what I can give her as the zeros in my head continue to pump me up with oxygen.

She uses her hand to pull herself away from her cart and toward me. At a foot away and a foot shorter, she looks me up and down. From here, her cloudy eyes look even greyer, and I can feel her sizing me up for who knows what.

"Can I tell you a secret?" Saliva jumps from her teeth and narrowly misses me.

"What kind of secret?" I wish my oily words were laced with as much confidence as they sound like they have.

"The secret to saving the world."

How is a person supposed to respond to that? I wish Stark were back, so he could finish loading up this woman's cart and help her get the fastest ticket out of this place.

"The secret is, art will save us all."

"Art will save us all." I'm aware I sound like I'm in a trance, like I'm robotically repeating what I hear. I just can't functionally make sense of what she's telling me or why. I guess I'm hoping if I hear them outloud with my own voice I can decode their meaning.

"That's right, young lady. Art is the key to everything. It's just a matter of getting it into the right hands so that the brilliant messages we need to listen to are actually heard." She takes a breath, then stares back up at me. I wonder if she can see those zeros that are still circling in my head. "You seem like a smart young lady, so I need you to promise me something, okay?"

"Sure." Anything that will make this person get on her way. Out the door. Adios.

"Promise me that when those messages come your way, you'll hear them, okay? Actually make an effort to hear what they are. Because the world needs to understand. It needs to know how to enter the future with open eyes and an open mind. And the only way to do that is to hear those messages. And that's especially true for those who aren't able to create for themselves. True for people like you, who are aware of it, too. So, please, listen when you can."

Before I can even think about how to respond, Stark comes back up to the front of the store with a handful of blisterpacks in the crook of his arm.

"Here you are, ma'am." He throws them into her cart for her. "I found another pack the system didn't even register. So consider it on the house."

Her eyes don't break from mine as she backs up and accepts Stark's offering. It's not until she's rolling out the doors and leading him to her car that I feel her magnetic grip break from me.

000 Blackwell Avenue. It's still ringing in my ears, as if knowing it is the key to saving the world, like she said.

CHAPTER TWELVE

Noland

It's sad to think about how temporary this room is for us. It just feels right being here together, sharing the same square footage, breathing in the same air, waking up to see each other first thing in the morning after a tired day. It's like we're playing house, just me and her as the close family members we should be.

I admit, letting her sleep was a mistake. I was supposed to keep her awake by keeping myself awake. We were supposed to watch each other with dreary eyes and heavy heads throughout the night. We were supposed to save ourselves for the entirety of the next day. Allowing my eyelids to close and drifting off to sleep was a mistake. If The Dignitary finds out, we may be in trouble. I won't let her find out. And I'm doubtful Mills will have any one-on-ones with The Dignitary to tip her off.

My chest tightens. Even worse than tipping off the one person who has a say in what happens to our future is the fact that soon, Mills and I will be forced to separate. It won't be long before we say goodbye to this room and our coexistence together. Such a shame because we could really make something of this place. Everything we need is right here. Our little kitchenette, a dining table, a pretty scenery right outside the window, and a bed.

My mind drifts a little to what could be done on that bed. Between the covers. To grab what's left of her talent for myself. But I can't. I pat my back pocket. That's where I've decided to keep my appreciation letter. I can't take any more of her talent. Not another ounce of it. Not yet. My restraint is needed. It's appreciated. And I'm not going to dirty up the image I'm building in The Dignitary's eyes. I can't risk that. Not anymore than I might have done already. No more mistakes.

Forget the bed. Forget anything that might have happened within it and on it and between the sheets with myself and any female form, but especially her. Because we're onto phase two, where we'll get onto Circle level, have our designated places, and work silently to speak with Dali da Monet and ascend to the realm we're meant to be in. We'll leave all the banals behind and enter where it's beautiful.

I don't know how long she's been standing here, staring at me. I imagine she has a lot of questions she refuses to ask. That's okay. She's always been a little stubborn, which is part of why I love her. I try to read her expression. Her face is stoic, plain, a little resolved and that is good. That means while she's heard pieces of the truth before, she's ready to start accepting them as part of her.

She walks over to the bay window and takes in the scenery. It really is beautiful out there with freshly cut grass and well cared for flower beds. There's a fresh stump where a pine tree used to be. I breathe in the memory of it. I know that each molecule of its existence was meant for us, for MMS.

I want to walk up behind her, wrap my hands around that tiny waist, and pull her in toward me. I want to rake my fingers through her messy hair and fix it into her signature pigtail braids. I want to feel where she keeps her talent and let it out into the open so I can grab it.

But I swallow back those feelings and instead ask her, "You know, Mills, everything you need is all here." I sit down at the little table. "We're here to care for you, Mills. And the others. We really do want the best for you."

Her hand lifts up. Between two perfect fingers is paper. A love letter with the Memento Mori seal on it. That must have been what the No Name gave her. Already, she's getting a love letter. Already, she's being praised for who she is.

I chose right, and that letter is proof.

"Do you really believe they want the best from me?" She turns her face around to meet my eyes. "Do you really want the best for me? Or is it just what's best for you? What you want?"

"For us." There's no hesitation. This is for us. For all of us. For me and her and us, us, us.

"Then tell me what this means." Her arm extends out with the offer of the letter. I tried to keep mine secret. Usually, love letters are meant just for the eyes of the person it's addressed to. But I guess in this case, when we're so close, I can have a glimpse. I can look. It's not like there's a rule against that. Not an explicitly stated one anyway.

The letter feels perfect. It's soft, just like mine was. And yet, when I pull it from her grip, it feels heavier somehow. Like it knows I'm about to read the words and it's sad about it. It unfolds easily and the words are exposed, the message naked. I suck in a breath and prepare myself for taking it in.

Dear: Ms Ellis,

We know you're confused right now. We see that, and we appreciate your understanding and endurance. It's not always easy adjusting to a new lifestyle, and yet you've done so well thus far.

At Memento Mori, we see artists like you and we know that underneath all the apprehension and confusion, you have what it takes to be one of the greats. The paintings you submitted are outstanding, and your eye for composition is better than most who have studied the art of art for decades. It truly is amazing what you can do.

However, after your moment in the paper room, we have some cause for concern. The other recruits all created something from nothing. They found ways to morph their mâché into large cylindrical shapes, include tiny details, and expand their horizons with the medium presented in front of them.

Your…sword… is a disappointment. We were hoping for more, Emily Ellis. We were sure you were able to do more, but even Michelangelo lapsed judgment once in a while.

Iris Mori
MMS Dignitary

So, not a love letter. A displeasure letter. How disappointing.

"Mills, I—"

"Cuz this doesn't sound like they want the best for me. Or maybe I'm not the best for them. And if that's the case," she crosses her arms at me, "then I don't know what the hell I'm doing here."

She's adorable. And sad. I want to scoop her up and cradle away her frustrations. But I have my own. This isn't how things were supposed to go. This was supposed to be a love letter, like mine. "Mills, you can't let some silly words on paper get you down." But I see my own words aren't cracking her surface. "Mills, you just have to try again. That's all. You just have to do better next time, do something great. Really blow them out of the water." There. That's what has to happen now. She just needs to get it together. Move forward. Push on.

Her face squinches up. It's like she's contemplating her choices in front of her and she's pinching out any options that don't make sense. But there's only one option. And that option is to do better. End of story.

I shake my head at her. "This is what's best for us, because it's what is best for you, too. This is an opportunity for you to learn and grow, do better. You're one of us now, Mills. You're part of the Memento Mori. All you need to do is accept it. Allow it to happen. And I promise you, what's best for us *is* what's best for you."

"I am not one of you." Her gaze has not broken from whatever she's staring at out the window. I can't imagine what she would be dreaming about looking out that sheet of glass. Everything she can see from here, it's all part of this, of us. It's put there for our enjoyment and pleasure.

I give her an understanding nod. "I know it doesn't feel like that now, Mills. Trust me. I was really hesitant at first, too. But I know if I continue doing what I need to do, then I'll have it all. Everything I need. Not just for now, on this plane, but forever, until past the end of time."

She turns herself away from the window and addresses me head on. This is the Mills I love. The feisty girl who doesn't shy away. "You said we have everything we need already." Already I can tell her words and tone are teetering between apprehension and acceptance. It's not going to take much to push her allegiance to where it needs to be.

I shake my head because, clearly, she didn't hear everything I said the first time. "Everything that we need *now*. On this plane of existence. But, love. There's so much more that our souls need, don't you understand?"

I stand up from my place and hug myself. I know if I don't touch my own skin, I'll end up giving up my restraint to hers. "You have to understand, Mills. You have to. You've said it before that your soul can't stop creating. It's a part of you that needs to be let out. Well, here, we all have souls like that. And for those of us who are able to hone it all in, there's a place for those souls to go. Not just to simply exist as a blip, but to be free. To soar. To be accepted and loved and respected as the masters of artistry, like our ancestors before us."

She stares me down. I can tell she's trying to come up with some retort. She's quiet. Nothing is coming to her. Again, another good sign.

"So, yes, for now, you have everything you need. You have a room with a view. You have the support of a strong system. You have someone willing to guide and lead you. And you have the love of…" I fight the urge to inch closer to her. "You have the love of a family who believes in you. And I believe in you to really astonish in the next task."

I take a step back from her because I know if I don't force myself backward, my feet will leap forward on their own.

"That's what we are, Mills. We're family here." I hope against hope she sees and understands what I'm trying to tell her because if she does, the next part of all this is going to be so much easier.

"I have a family already."

Oh how I wish her words were true. But they're not. She's told me what her "family" has been like in the past. It's not family at all. Just a single mom who turned a blind eye every time Mills decided to walk away.

"Oh, Mills." I give her the best understanding look I can muster. "You know that's not the same. Even now, what has your mother done? When was the last you talked with her? At most, I'm sure she thinks you're off doing the same thing you've always done. Run away. Run away to something else only to come back later. Am I right?" I pause, hoping for a response, but she doesn't give me one. "Only this time, you didn't even have to run. We found you. We've taken you in. And now, we're caring for you. And no one here will ignore your whereabouts."

When she still doesn't respond, I swallow and attempt to dull down my words. "At least that's what I hope you end up seeing us as, Mills. We want to be the family you've never had."

She nearly spits at me. But she doesn't because she's starting to understand. And she wants to do better. This was a student who never backed down from a challenge. And I was her professor to push her into doing whatever she needed to do to overcome whatever hurdles those challenges threw her way.

"This is where we tell you that your talent and your painting, your skill, your drive, the canvases you touch, and the heart that goes into it all… it's all deathly important. I know you've never heard that before. Not really. Not to this extent."

I lick my lips to make sure the next piece comes out right. "So, Mills, I know you may not believe it now. But if you give me — if you give us a chance, I can promise you'll see being here is a good thing. And you can't quit now just because this letter isn't…"

"A love letter. Like yours."

I nod. "Exactly." Though, I hate that her curiosity forced her to read it.

There's a growling sound that comes from her body, and I want to kneel on the floor and wrap myself around her waist. I want to place my lips on her belly button and suck the sound away because that sound means hunger. And hunger means pain. But, instead, I smile. "Mills, I promise you have everything you need."

It's all I can say before there's a knock on the door. My eyes widen in excitement and nerves. If this is what I think it is, then phase two is starting a lot sooner than I expected.

I crack the door open and see a man — a No Name. It's what we call all those who hold no real position or purpose for the next realm. Their entire existence is sadly here, in this reality, doing all the little jobs around the facility. No Names are the janitors and groundskeepers. They're the staff who cook and clean and have a small understanding of what we're doing here. They're paid by the hour for the work but don't take part in anything really meaningful to our cause. Yet, they see our artistic expressions and appreciate them all the same.

But this No Name? He just rang the bell to kickstart phase two.

"Here you are, sir," he tells me as he hands over a hot air balloon made out of paper mâché.

"Thank you," I tell him, and close the door.

Mills furrows her eyebrows. "That's not mine." Her voice is staticy, like she barely has control over how the sound is coming out.

"I know it's not, love. But that's the point."

I take the hot air balloon over to the table. Then I help myself into the supply cabinets. I pull out all the paint I can find, even the redundant hues that have no business being there. I don't want anything to hold her back from her own brilliance. The tiny bottles make clinking sounds as I spread them out on the table into a neatly lined pattern. "The point is, the support network I've been talking about, the family here? We're building it together."

A slight push adjusts the hot air balloon within Mills's reach. "And right now, you're here to help build that family. We want to see how well you can build on someone else's work. See if you can pick up where someone else left off, and improve upon it with your own artistic eye. This is your chance, Mills. Show us what you have."

With hesitant hands, she picks up the paper mâché and moves it around to observe. "You want me to paint this?" The tiny glint in her eyes fills me with excited butterflies. There she is. The painter I adore.

I nod, but allow the silence around us to fill our ears. I need her to feel how important this is. I need her to accept the challenge and prove to the entire MMS that my choice was the right choice. Because it's all part of the plan.

Her stomach growls again. "If I paint this thing, will you bring me some food? Maybe some water?"

My lip tastes salty when I bite into it. "I promise, you have everything you need," I say as I walk toward the door.

"That doesn't answer my question." I swear, she gets punchier by the day.

I find the button next to the door and hover my finger over it. "It answers everything," I assure her.

Then I press the button. Static erupts from speakers in every corner of the room, and The Dignitary's voice fills any voice of silence left.

"You have until tonight." The door opens and the No Name man is still standing there, doing his duty. I nod to acknowledge him. He smiles, happy to watch over this door until given the orders to leave.

"Noland, will you bring me food then? Tonight? Answer me!"

But I can't answer. Because anything I have to say isn't nearly as important as what Mills needs to hear. The teachings of Memento Mori Society. They'll be drilled into her consciousness all day as she paints, until we're ready for the next phase.

CHAPTER THIRTEEN

Mills

"Memento Mori Society is a proud family who is honored to witness your accomplishments. We know how important your art is to you and we are here to support that and the talent that comes with it. We are building our family from the ground up full of those who inspire us to be the artists our souls push us to be. You have the opportunity to help build this family as you see fit. As a network. As a system to rely on. As an educational and spiritual backbone that leans on everything you love. We see you. We love you. We want to experience you through your artistic expression. The work you do is so important to us because we know how important it is to you."

It's only been a few minutes, but I've already memorized the speech. It's like it's dug its way under my skin and is swimming in my veins. I'll never get it out of my system. It sounds ridiculous and yet at the same time, it sounds completely reasonable. It's a fight within me that doesn't feel like there will ever be a winning side.

"Ahhh!"

I pick up a jar of paint and throw it across the room. It hits the wall. Blue splatters across it and, honestly, this room has never looked better. I pick up another and throw it in another direction. Pink shatters everywhere, but it's not even satisfying because I can't hear the glass over the sound of this woman in the speakers. Purple goes in one direction and green goes in another. De-sterilizing the walls feels like relief and guilt all wrapped up in the same ball of emotion. And when I take a moment to breathe, my throat feels dry.

The button. I run over to the door and push it in with my thumb. The same stupid button Noland pressed to start this mess. For some reason, I think things really could be that easy, that I could just willy-nilly press a button and the confusion would stop. I'd have the silence to think about what I've been told, how I feel, and to decipher what's real and what's not. But things can never be so easy. I press it and nothing happens. Again, I press. Nothing. I jam my finger over and over on that little button and still, the woman isn't skipping a beat in delivering her speech to my ears.

But the door. It's right there. Duh. And there's no way Noland could lock it from the outside, right? Even with a dizzy head, I know this much. I mean, I could easily let myself out before. At least, I could open the door. Had that *doctor* not been waiting there like some kind of murdery creep, I would have been free as a bird then, ready to flap my wings and fly away.

Was he a murdery creep? He did load up Noland with healing cream. Because of him, the burns on my face feel nonexistent.

I do want to leave, right? It is still what I want. Right?

I close my eyes, whisper, "God, please let it be unlocked," and twist. Thank Frida Kahlo, it moves! The door opens, and a rush of air has never smelled so sweet. Of course a few days without food might actually make anything smell good.

That is, until I'm greeted by a giant, burly man. He has a name tag on and yet, no name is on it. Figures. I smile at him. He smiles at me. Then I put on my sticky sweet kindness voice and say, "Hi. I think there's been a mistake. I'm supposed to go home now." Maybe he's the kind of guard who has a kind and understanding heart. Maybe he sees that I'm confused and concerned and home is where a girl just like me needs to iron it all out.

My hopes are shattered when he says, "Ma'am, you are home."

I am home. The sound of those words rattling in my head makes sense. This is home. This is where I'm accepted and loved and supported and welcomed. It's where I've been brought in with open arms. Home. This is home, right?

I shake my head. I'm not getting anywhere with that. Time for a new tactic. "I'm sorry. I meant, I really have to go pee. Like, really bad. Could I please use the restroom?"

He cocks his head to the side, confused. So my nerves push it a little more, testing the limits of my own made up story.

"I really need to go. It's *lady issues*."

He cocks his head a little further and opens his mouth in an "O" shape. That's right, Mr. *I don't have a name on my nametag.* Now you have to let me out so I can use the bathroom.

But he points back into my room. "Toward the right. Last door. Menstruation products are available under the vanity."

Of course. In all the confusion and frustration and reluctance, I miscalculated that lie. There is a bathroom in here. It's where I was cleansed in the ice bath Noland prepared for me.

Which means water.

I'm sure my eyes go wide like saucers as I slam the door on the man in front of me. I don't care. It doesn't matter. Neither do any of the other matching men I saw lining the hallway guarding the doors.

And I run to the bathroom.

When the door swings open, I'm welcomed with a beautiful image. The sink. The perfect sink with a tap that might as well be made of gold. My hand reaches the cold faucet like a magnet and turns. My mouth reaches underneath and I suck in as much water as I can. I'm hungry for it and allow the cold liquid to run over my lips and splash on my cheeks. It feels amazing. Refreshing. Like a cleanse.

A cleanse.

I allow myself to drink my fill, filling my stomach until it hurts. Maybe I'll store it like a camel. Maybe not. It doesn't really matter, anyway, because this satisfies any hunger I might have felt. This will be good for now.

"To be the artists our souls push us to be."

Again, the thought passes me by: a cleanse.

I have been full of doubt and reluctance. But what was it that Noland said? The same thing that Zak and Paula echoed? Something about the banals. The borings. Noland told me the first cleanse was short, shorter than it should have been. The idea is crazy, but maybe a second, longer cleanse might clear my head.

It did feel like it cleared me the first time around.

It would definitely feel good against my skin.

The bathtub porcelain is cold. So cold, it was almost sterile. But I'm choosing to accept it as welcoming instead. As if it's been waiting for me, the chained plug is hanging over the faucet. I grab it, feel its weight, and gingerly place it over the drain. With a deep inhale, I start the cold water.

It rushes like a waterfall, and I almost feel giddy at the sight. I want to dip my toes in and swim like a fish. I want to drink it like a fish, too. But I remind myself that I can't get greedy. My stomach already feels like it's about to pop like a balloon.

But even though the water rushing from the faucet is cold, I know it's not cold enough.

Shit.

I'm about to hate this part.

The little kitchenette is right around the corner. And even though I know there's nothing to eat inside the fridge, I'm willing to bet —

Yup. The freezer door swings open and there's a mountain of ice in the bin inside.

Fan-freaking-tastic.

But it is really good. It's what I wanted, needed, right? Gosh, I sound like a crazy person. But, crazy is as crazy does, so I shrug my shoulders and dive in. The ice bin is heavy and every step I take closer to the bathroom has me second and triple guessing what the hell I'm doing. Every time an ice cube drops from my grip, it skids across the floor. Just another piece of uncertainty ready to melt away.

Dumping the ice into the tub isn't difficult. Just slips on out and makes a sickening rush of *plopplopplopplop* sound. Yet, it doesn't even seem like it's that much. Definitely not as much as before. But, it'll do. It'll have to do.

The tap turns off and before I can quadruple guess myself, I wriggle out of my jeans and let them drop to the floor. Then goes my underwear, my shirt, and the sweaty bra. I stink. Judging by the not-so-love note, I stink in multiple ways.

It's time to wash off the boring. Wash off the stink.

My skin prickles at the instant chill. The spiked sensation momentarily blocks out the voice blaring over the speakers. This is good. This means I can focus. It's not as bad as before. Not as painful. Maybe it's because I'm not in even half the amount of ice as before. But maybe it's because I'm cleaning off what I need. Maybe it's doing the trick. Maybe I'm doing it right.

I sit like this for as long as I can, numbing my nerves and blanking my mind. Whatever I do next needs to be better. My next move needs to impress.

It's a good thing the next thing is painting. I can rock the shit out of that. I better not screw up the thing I'm best at.

The way my body expands when I breathe in reminds me of the balloon waiting for me. I watch it go. Breathe in, and out goes my stomach. Ice cubes rush from the center and scatter to the sides of the tub. And when I breathe out, everything collects again. It's little waves that pool in and around me, making me wonder about how Paula's hot air balloon might fly in the wind. Maybe pieces of it would expand in and out, too. Maybe Paula's Nana would like that.

When the ice finally melts, my heartrate settles. My body heat feels like it's warming up and my fingers and toes feel like little raisins at the end of my digits. Time to come out. My makeshift cleansing is done. I hope it's enough.

It better freaking be enough.

"We want to experience you through your artistic expression."

The moment I break free of the water, the woman's voice is back. I'm back in reality. A voice in the back of my mind questions if reality even exists anymore.

Fine. I put my stinky clothes back on and drag my feet back to the main room. With wet skin and blasting air conditioning, I feel even colder than in my cleanse.

My stomach tenses. It reminds me of my last request from Noland. Food. But that request is no longer necessary because I've already filled it to the brim.

Everything I could possibly need, right?

"Memento Mori is a proud family."

Everything? Really? Even free will and choice?

"Build this family as you see fit."

I want in, but I want out. I can't choose either, and any choice I actually have is impossible.

"The people you always needed to love and support you."

The recorded phrases dig even deeper under my skin and worm their way into my brain. They scratch at it, creating little homes to live in permanently. I fall to the floor and cradle myself, trying to stop it from happening. My hands create earmuffs over my ears and I close my eyes, but it's no use. There's no ignoring what's happening around me and to me. These messages are right, aren't they? I've always wanted a place to belong and be seen. I've always wanted somewhere to allow my artistic expression to run wild, push the limits, and create something that's never been put out there before.

So I sit. I cry. I let hot tears find their way out into the open. And I think of that hot air balloon and Paula.

Poor Paula who lost her Nana. Poor Paula who watched it happen. Poor Paula who created a hot air balloon because it's what reminded her of the one piece of family she had.

Until now.

When my body can no longer bear to sit in the same place for longer, I push myself off the floor and over to the table. I pull out a chair and look at what's in front of me. Sure, I killed off a few jars of paint, but there's still plenty to work with in front of me.

I have all day to hone in my craft, to use my artistic expression.

I open a jar and paint. One stroke after another, ensuring not a single one is boring, banal.

And as I paint, I think about how I can support Paula, be the encouragement she's always wanted. Because that's what family members do.

CHAPTER FOURTEEN

Mills

My hands are covered in colorful freckles. Pigments of reds and blues and purples dot my skin like I stuck my hand in a confetti jar and pulled out a new set of hands I wasn't born with. This is what good art feels like, so immersed into what I was doing I couldn't pay attention to how much of what color got on me or my clothes. Not that it matters that my clothes are covered in paint. They're so full of grime, this is an improvement.

The recorded message is still going. The Dignitary's voice is still churning her words, but I can't even make them out anymore. They're just kinda mush in my subconscious. They're there, but I can't exactly grab hold of them and do anything with them. They're just weird noodly thoughts now.

The bay window is dark. I can barely make out the flowerbeds through the blue haze. Guess I made it through the day, right? The thought pulls me into a fit of giggles. Another day gone and I'm still standing. Two days? Three? Four? Time doesn't make sense

I made it. I got through the day, painting left and right, and even though the walls around me are splattered into imperfection, I'm here. Still standing.

I laugh a little more. Muffled, but it's there.

Here I am, just this lost little girl who wanted to find her way out of this place. And yet, what did I spend my time doing? Painting. My laughter escapes into

the open, loud enough I can hear it puncture through the recorded message. I just spent an entire day doing the exact thing they wanted me to do. And why? Because it is actually the thing I love to do. It's what I wanted to do, too. Because they get it. Because this is the place that really does understand and hold artistic expression so valuable that they'd create an entire space just for it.

My belly cramps up as I double over and my cheeks do that weird pinching thing when I'm trying to hold back even more barking chuckles. It's so funny, I can't stop, and my laughter and the recorded message are tangled up in the air together as one. Music is what it is. And the more I hear my laughter as the backdrop to the recorded melody, the funnier it becomes. I cannot stop. And I kind of love it.

That is, until my giggles swirl behind my eyes and make me dizzy. I overdid it. And without any more water in my stomach, it wants something in its place. But I can't do anything about it now. Guess my stomach will have to work on the acid inside of it to tie it over. There are more important things on my plate now.

I take a look at the hot air balloon on the table. I wonder what Paula would say about it. If this is what she had in mind: an old wooden door wrapping around the entire parachute. Each panel marking a new grain pattern. And in the front, a giant lock, rusted closed in reds and oranges. The chords and skirt connecting the basket extends the locked door in cage-like bars. And the basket underneath holds the one thing needed to break free. It is the key, painted in gold and silver. It's riding within the cage, by the door, so close and yet entirely too far to actually break out.

I exhale my last giggle and focus my concentration. That's exactly where I am now. I could open up the door to this room, but I'll never be allowed to just walk out. And the weird thing is? It makes absolute sense. This place is providing me the space and time to do what I love. And everyone here is encouraging it in a way that makes me want to do more. It's not about if I'll get a good paying job or if it's "worth it" in the end. It's not about a cute hobby that's reserved for pockets of free time. It is about having a space to explore the provided creative outlet.

I pick up the mâché balloon. Maybe the door I've been locked behind doesn't belong to the room I'm in. Maybe the lock is actually everyone outside of this building who has pigeonholed the idea of art being a silly form of guilty pleasure. Fun, but ultimately without any value.

Just then, the recording stops. It's eerily quiet. The voice that has been with me for hours has completely disappeared, and yet the ghost of it is still ringing in my ears, their half truths turning full.

The door cracks open. I don't even need to look up to know it's Noland. He is my handler, after all. My number one supporter and fan. He is my guide and teacher. And if Memento Mori can praise him for holding me accountable and keeping himself to a high standard, then I think I can accept him as a part of this family we're creating together.

"You are amazing." His voice sounds proud, and for a moment, I'm shot back to the days when I worked for that approval. Now, I know I don't even have to work for it. I've earned it fair and square. I'll never have to work for his approval again.

He joins me at the table, marveling over my work on top of Paula's work. I wonder which object she was given. If she had Zak's lion or my machete or any one of the other pieces made just the other day. I guess it doesn't matter as long as she had the chance to play with her talent, too.

"Simply amazing," he reiterates. Then, his eyes move to meet mine and his tone shifts from adoration to seriousness.

"I have no concerns for you tonight, Mills."

No? Why would he?

"Everything you've done up to now holds this level of dedication and genius. The work you've created is enough. At least for me it is." Then, he swallows. His hands reach across the table to find mine. I let them.

They're shaky, as if he is trying to hold back his touch. But they're also warm and comforting. It feels nice.

"But tonight isn't about me or you. It's about the bigger picture. It's about The Circle."

I nod, as if I understand what that means. In a way, I do, even though I've never fully been told what The Circle is or how important it may be.

"The Circle has a space for five people. Well, ten. Five handles who have brought in the utmost talent to offer. And the five people who have been their recruits. Mills, I aim to be one of those people. And I hope you can be, too. Because The Circle is who gets to move on to the realm beyond this one."

"Beyond this realm?" I want to understand, I really do.

"Yes; beyond this realm people call reality. But, Mills, this isn't the reality we're supposed to live in. There's a whole other realm beyond that knows the value in creativity. It's where we can relax and love and be who we are. And art is the most powerful tool to express all of that, don't you believe? Isn't that what I taught you?"

I nod, even though it's not something I think he taught me. It's something I was born knowing, as all artists are. He was just the person to help me inhabit the tools to carry that truth out. I appreciate that he's always been the person to encourage me.

He nods, too. "I'm so glad that you're starting to understand how important this all is." He squeezes my hands. "Mills, tonight is so important. Tonight, we go to the gallery. We present your artwork, and then we wait. There will be judgment. People are going to decide which recruits have the most to offer. You do understand you're a recruit, right?"

I nod again. Yes. I am a recruit. I was put here to do my thing and let it carry him and me and us into the next thingie. Realm? Yeah, that thing.

"Good. They're going to judge your paintings against all the other recruits, and I have no doubt that yours is going to outshine the rest, Mills. But here's the thing, the public will be there, too. People who don't fully understand what we're about. They're going to browse around, maybe point out a few things they like, and then they'll walk away forgetting what they saw. Some people might go so far as to buy a piece or two. But here's what I need you to remember. You cannot interact with them, okay?"

"Noland?" I squeeze his hands back, soaking in their warmth. I need him to know that I'm not an idiot. I absolutely understand the importance of this. It's pretty obvious. And if this is important to him and Memento Mori, then it's important for the sake of art. It's important for the world. But I don't understand why I can't wave hello to someone outside of our growing family. Wouldn't it make more sense to do something like, oh I don't know, educate them? "Why not? Why can't we interact with other people?"

Noland frowns. "Mills, they aren't going to understand. Not yet anyway." He lets go of my hands, and now mine feel cold without his touch. "But their time will come, I promise. We will share the importance of our work eventually. But we need to ensure we have the strongest artists to do so, first. We need to have the right voices behind our cause. Then, and only then, will we be able to share with the world the importance of who we are and the creations our imaginations give birth to."

He swallows again. "Look, tonight isn't about the world around us. It's about us and the importance of the next step. So, tonight, I need you to sit back and just let it happen. Let your art speak for you. Let it speak for all of us, and for itself. There's enough power in it to do that tonight. And then, we move on. We learn more. We educate more."

As I nod again, my eyes drift to the walls I splattered earlier. Guilt fills me up like a kid who has scribbled on the walls when her daddy wasn't looking. That guilt must have leaked out into the open, because Noland addresses me again.

"Don't worry about the walls, Mills. That's just a part of your process. You had to go through that to create this." He gestures to the hot air balloon between us. "Besides, I think it looks better than it did before." He gives me a smile, then pulls out something from behind him.

The mask. The one of my face. The one that made me woozy before.

"Think you're ready for this?" he asks me.

I suck in my cheeks, unsure of how to respond.

"It's just for tonight. Everyone will wear one. Look," he pulls out a second one, "even me. All of us. We're in this together, Mills. Ready?"

I consider the art in front of me. The paper mâché I created earlier. My paintings that are no doubt already hanging in the gallery, including the ones that should have been eaten up in the fire. "For the sake of art?" I ask.

He nods. "For the sake of art."

I nod. If that's the case, "Then I'm ready."

CHAPTER FIFTEEN

Livvy

I try to rub away the jitters on my arms. "Stark, I'm nervous."

We need to visit Blackwell. And the time will come to go exploring on their grounds, but there is no passing up the gallery. We have to be here. Way before any of this, we promised Mills, and I'm not breaking my promise to her. Ever. Besides, what if we find something that leads us to her? What if we find Mills herself?

I hang onto my brother's arm. I don't know what to expect once those doors unlock. Will Mills's paintings be hanging on the wall? Including the ones that were stowed away in the alcove? Will there be some semblance of her there? Or is her entire identity going to be wiped clean of the place?

"I'm nervous, too, sis." He gives me a little shove, "But can I tell you something else? I'm also a little excited."

I give him a few jerky nods and myself a few "Wooo-sah"'s to calm down. I suppose a part of my jitters might be excitement, too. Maybe Mills will be inside, just waiting for us to join her. She'll be all smiles with a crazy story to tell, but otherwise scratch and scar free. One could hope. I'd be relieved. Mad that she didn't let me in on whatever she was doing, but relieved.

He bends down to my ear and says loud enough for me to hear, "You said it yourself, Liv. She's gotta be alive, right? And she might just be behind these doors."

A few more jerky nods. I hope my gut and cognition hasn't failed me on this.

"Ladies and gentlemen!" a woman's voice calls over the crowd.

I can't tell where she's coming from until I see two wrinkled hands shoot up in the air, waving frantically. When her linen sleeves fall away from her hands, I can see that one wrist adorns a purple band. "Ladies and gentlemen!" she says again, and when the crowd still doesn't respond in unison, she pulls her hands back down and out of sight.

Within seconds, she pops up out of the crowd and into the air. I see a head of dyed red hair with silver roots and thick lens glasses. It's her. The lady who was judging us harder than Judith Blum herself at Craft Your Pants art supply store. What is she doing here? She wobbles a bit and I can see the back of a chair behind her. I don't know where that chair came from, but it arrived as quick as she did. I guess the people here come prepared and ready for what she needs at a whim.

"Ladies and gentlemen," she calls for a third time, and this time, the crowd turns to her, ready to hear her speech. I inch a little closer, dragging Stark with me so we can hear, too.

"Today is a special day. Today, we open up the doors to the Volga community and allow you to embrace the artistic side of our imaginations. It's a little wild, a little eccentric, and a little breathtaking. But I can promise you one thing, you haven't seen anything like this yet in the town of Volga."

An eruption of clapping sounds off from one side of the crowd and ripples over to the other. The wrinkled lady waves her hands in excitement for a moment, then she stops their movement, conducting the crowd to quiet down, and they oblige.

"But before I swing these doors wide open, we have some rules. There will be no touching of any of the artworks. Even the ones you find extra enticing, please keep your hands off. That is, unless you'd like to purchase them. In that case, touch away and watch your money go toward a very noble cause: to a society of artists who are changing the world at their fingertips."

She takes a breath, then continues. "Please make sure you move through in a timely manner. No gawking for long periods, clogging up the hallways. Everyone wants to be able to see the exhibits at hand, so please make sure you keep things moving along nicely. You may see some things that are… interesting. That doesn't mean you should impede the foot traffic or dirty it up with your touch. Some of the more interesting exhibits cannot accept your fingertips, even if you have the money to purchase them."

Here, she stops again. I can't see her eyes behind her thick lenses, but I assume she's using them to scan the crowd for reactions. There aren't any which are relevant. The citizens of Volga are simply waiting their time before they can spend a Saturday doing something that breaks from their routine of mundane groceries and bills.

"We're excited to bring you an entirely new segment guaranteed to make you think and question the things around you. It should. It should be provocative and entertaining. It should get you excited. It should make you gasp and wonder what reality means and what messages you should bring home. I really hope you're able to open your mind to what's in front of you and the messages it may give you. And, of course, I hope you enjoy. Again, keep in mind not to touch anything on display. Got it? Keep your hands to yourself!"

Messages to bring home? Her words here echo her words from the store. That connection definitely has me more intrigued than almost anything else that might be behind those closed doors. Almost.

There is a share of nods and one man shouts, "Just open the doors already! It's hot!"

He's not wrong, but I cringe at the fact that this outburst is a core representation of the people out here. Just wanting to gawk at something inside a comfortable air-conditioned building on a Saturday afternoon. There's nothing better to do in this town, so they're all collecting here to see what the excitement is all about.

"Yes," this lady says, and I can hear in her voice she is annoyed, too. The way her lips part just slightly, I wonder if she would much rather keep the doors shut to keep out the public riffraff. I also wonder what Mills would think about this pint-sized gatekeeper.

"We will open the doors in three, two," she inhales for dramatic effect, "one." Two men in all linen open the front doors, and the crowd files in like cattle. Stark and I are just two bovines trotting along, squished shoulder to shoulder, the atoms in our bodies heating up against the atoms touching our skin. It's sticky. And it's gross.

We shuffle along until the air conditioning hits our skin and the scent of pine hits our noses, a reprieve from the bodily heat everyone is sharing. And once we walk through those doors, the crowd disperses. A few people turn left, as if they're going to browse the artwork the same way they read a page in a book. Others turn right, going against the grain of natural instinct. Stark and I plow forward. We have our eyes set on one thing and one thing only.

To find Mills's paintings.

Each strip of wall has a set of paintings, little spotlights shining on them. One features some kind of blocky stuff that's hard to make out. The paintings feel stale, like whoever made them measured out every line exactly with a straight-edge ruler. They don't have the organic feeling of Mills's. We keep moving.

Another row is full of pretty flowers and trees. Something I could see hanging in my grandmother's hallway, collecting dust because she refused to ever replace it. Our feet continue to move. Row after row, I don't see anything familiar until, finally, I do.

I see Mills's paintings. All five of them. Including the two with the burned edges Stark and I found in the melted clock house.

I see the one that looks like Starry Night, but through a victim's eyes, with her assailant looming over her. I see the one that looks like The Girl With the Pearl Earring, except the girl's face is in horror, terrified of her last moments. I see the one that started it all. The one that resembles The Scream, only even more graphic and provocative. The only reason why I know any of these references are because of Mills. Even though I've never fully understood it, even though I could never work a brush the way I can a microscope, I learned from her. I learned that each painting holds a piece of the artist themselves, and I can feel Mills through each of these. It's like she's speaking to me, beyond the subjects on canvas, beyond the layer of paint, and even beyond her intention of bringing the focus to the victims found in the Volga community.

I feel her message. The one that so desperately wants to be heard and seen. Mills doesn't want to be overlooked herself, either. Is this what I'm supposed to bring home with me? Is this the message I'm supposed to find?

Stark is standing in front of the last painting. The one that looks like a caged Mills, trapped and struggling. The look on his face tells me he's feeling just as weighted as I am. He's always appreciated good art. Years ago, he was the kind of person to keep a pencil in his back pocket just in case inspiration hit him and he needed to get it out of his system before it was gone for good. It's kind of why I connected so well to Mills in the first place. I saw my brother in her.

Well, kind of. I saw the same drive in her, the same fire behind her eyes.

And now, there's a fire back behind Stark's, and I know there's a special place he's making in his heart for the painting in front of him, too.

I really wish he would explore his own talent again. I wish he'd stop holding out on all of us, including himself. Maybe that's the message he's supposed to take away for himself. Because then maybe, one day, his art could be held up for display in a place like this, as well. Only, when that happens, he better be standing right next to me, proudly admiring his own artwork and not possibly held captive somewhere.

"Why?" Stark asks, and I watch his hand touch the burnt corner of the canvas.

"Why what?" is all I can respond with because there are a million whys I can think to ask right now.

Why are these paintings here? Why did Professor Elsinger go through the trouble to make sure they were displayed? Why did he disappear and go into hiding? Why are those men in linen working for him? Why is the crazy red-haired lady running this operation?

"Why is this one signed by him?"

That isn't a why I had considered, but sure enough, at the bottom corner is a different handwritten word that doesn't match the "Emily Ellis" on all the others.

It says: *Noland Elsinger.*

"Maybe he painted that one?" I suggest. Though, the idea of Noland planting himself in a dark basement to paint a canvas of entrapping Mills makes the acid in my stomach burn.

His hand goes back to the painting. He traces the outline of her face. It's like he wants to break the bars of the cage around her and set her free.

"That's not it," he says. "This doesn't feel like a stranger's painting. This feels like her. In fact it feels more like her than the others. This one feels way more personal.

"No. Touching," a man's voice sneaks up behind us. I turn around to see he's head to toe in the exact same linen get-up as damn near everyone else working for this gallery. Only this man is wearing a name tag.

"Hello my name is," and that's where it stops.

It's blank. There's nothing there. As if he doesn't have a name at all.

His eyes glare at us, and I wonder if he's been put here for a reason, too. To intimidate us? To entrap others? To do who knows what with the paintings on the wall?

"No. Touching," he says again, "unless you're ready to pay up for it. Then, touch it all you want. It's your grubby handprints on it, anyway."

"Fine. Deal." Stark puts his entire hand on the canvas, right in the middle, over Mills's heart. "I'll buy it."

The man's eyes grow wide as does his smile. "You just put down $3,000 my friend. Make out the check to the Memento Mori Society." And he walks away.

"Stark, do you have that kind of money?"

He shrugs. "That's what credit cards are for. It doesn't matter, though. It's coming home with me. A piece of Mills is coming home with me. And when we find Mills, I will make sure she has the chance to fix the signature on this. I can't let it go to someone else. What if they thought *he* was the mind behind this? That's just not right. She needs credit for her own work. Besides, I've always wanted an Emily Ellis original, and now, I guess I own one."

I let him soak in the ownership and have a look around the room, hoping for a sign, anything that might lead me in the next direction. And that's when I see it, at least twenty seats are filled across the room, all with people sitting still. All dressed in the same linen uniform. And all with their faces covered by a painted mask. Twenty pairs of vacant eyes all stare out in the same direction. One with a pair of tiny blue butterflies in the place of irises.

"Stark." I grab his arm and pull him away.

"Hm?" His attention is still on the painting.

"Stark," I say again. "Look."

He turns around, and his facial expression reads the same way I feel. Confused and terrified. And yet, there's a slight ounce of hope.

We inch our way over. I want to touch these people, comb through each of them and see if I can find one with Mills's blonde hair. Or her thin frame. Or her size nine shoes. But there's a line of men, all dressed the same, with the same blank name tags, all guarding the masked people in chairs. We can only get so close to them, and I take advantage of ever inch they allow for me to take toward them.

"Stark, she's here, isn't she?" My heart is thumping irregular, loud beats. I'm sure he can hear it, if his isn't just as loud.

He whispers back, "Would that be too easy?"

One of the men eyes us. He's following our conversation, so I guide Stark a few steps away from him, hoping to shrug his gaze off. "Look, I don't know who these people are or what they want to do with her, but I get the feeling that she's right here in front of our faces. And, no, it doesn't seem too easy. Do you see how many guards they have?"

Stark bites his lip as his eyes scan rapid darts along the crowd in front of us. This is difficult. If Mills is right here, how will we find her? I can't see anyone's face. Or hair. There's no telltale signs of who is who in front of us.

"Mills," I call, but not too loud. I don't want to draw attention to us. I just hope she can hear my voice and give me a sign. "Mills," I say a little louder when I don't see a single person move.

"Mills," Stark calls after me, even louder than I dare.

"Stark, she's here," I tell him. "She's got to be here."

And one of the figures moves, just barely. The one with butterfly eyes. Their hands move on their lap, palm up. And I can see burn marks. They're healing over, but they're there. Red splotches that could have come from anything. But if I had a guess, it would be from a fire.

My hand vise-grips Stark's arm, and I shoot him a look. Without saying a word, I tell him, "She's here. There she is. And we have to get her!"

My foot steps forward. I don't care if they told us to stand back, and I don't care if they told us not to touch anything. Stark touched something, and now he's three thousand dollars in the hole, but that's worth it because it's a part of Mills. Which means if all I need to do is bust through a few steps forward and grab Mills herself, then it's totally worth it. Even if they do make me purchase the entire "exhibit" to get her out. I'll pay ten thousand of what I don't have to do it. I'll push through each one of these men and grab her as my own. I'll go into debt for the rest of my life just to make sure she is okay and that she gets back in one piece.

A flip flopping stomach makes me realize I just put a number on my friend's head.

Stark and I both spring forward, ready to grab her. Only, the moment one of the guardsmen sees us is the same moment his arms are around me. And another man's arms are around Stark.

I kick. I scream. I yell. I even bite the man's shoulder. But all it does is tighten his grip on me. Every part of me squeezes under him and I do everything I can not to become a tube of toothpaste. My fit starts a commotion. All of Volga county turns to see who's throwing a tantrum, who has broken what rule to get escorted out. I don't care about that.

What I do care about is that the men who have us in their muscular arms are taking us away. Away from the crowd, away from the gallery, and away from Mills. I don't want the distance to grow any further. I've already lost her once and just when I barely found her, I'm losing her again.

"No! You can't do this!" I yell at them. "You have to let us see her!"

In my peripheral, Stark is fighting off just as much. He grunts and pulls and struggles, too. But the guy who holds him hostage in a vise-like grip is even bigger than my oaf.

Neither man addresses us with their words. Only stronger holds. And as we reach the doors, they open with ease and out we are in the heat again. Away from it all.

"The rules were no touching. You heard them. We all heard them. If you can't adhere to the rules, then we can't trust you with the displays in there."

"Breaking the rules? Bullshit!" I yell. And somehow all my insecurities have disappeared. I feel Mills within me, cheering me on, telling me to stop being so meek and mild when someone you love is on the line.

"He broke the rules and you didn't kick us out." I don't mean to throw Stark under the bus, but I'm not sure what else to say. There could have been a warning at least. Though, I suppose rationalizing with an oaf won't do me or Stark or Mills any good.

"He broke the rules on a regular display. One you can buy away. Which reminds me, we expect payment within twenty four hours. You broke the rules on a special display. You can't put a price on a person."

That flip-flop feeling is back again. Internally, I yell at myself for even thinking I might be able to purchase Mills out of this place. And yet, I also breathe out a little relief. At least whatever dark operation this is, they're not selling off humans.

With that, the doors close, but both men stare at us, daring us to go back in. Daring to test them yet again.

"Ughhh!" I stomp the ground and pinch my fists at my side. "Stark, that's not fair. She was right there. She was telling me something."

"Yeah, she was telling us she's okay."

"What?"

"That's what that meant. Her hands were gentle. It didn't feel angry. It didn't feel scared. It felt calm and collected. She's okay, Liv."

"She's okay?" I can't believe that. I refuse to believe that. How can she be okay?

“At least for now, Liv.”

Stark’s words ring in my ears. For now. But how long will okay last?

CHAPTER SIXTEEN

Mills

I had always thought seeing my own art in a gallery would be a pivotal point in my life. Like the birth of ipods making CDs extinct. Or when the floss became a dance and not just a dental hygiene recommendation. Yes, I said recommendation, and I stand by it. Flossing sucks. I figured being in a gallery would have been the stepping stone to ease my name into a few households, even if they were only local.

What I didn't expect was having it be *this* pivotal. I didn't expect it to be so serious. Not just my career on the line, but my life. My existence. My entire purpose for being on this crazy spinning planet. And even more so, the existence of everyone else. From my understanding, this right here is a moment that will affect the entire world, regardless if they understand the eyes of an artist or not.

I'm not sure I fully understand it myself. I hope more people do, though. Because the more who understand, the more likely the world will be saved.

I also never expected it to look like this, sitting still in a wooden chair next to Noland and surrounded by the handlers and recruits of Memento Mori. All clothed in linen jumpsuits, hoods over our hair, and masks to fit perfectly over the features that make up our faces. I won't lie, the fresh clothing feels good. And even though I can't see the people around me, I sense them all here. Somewhere within this collective breathing, Zak is sitting next to Jon. Paula is next to her handler. And all the others are lined up. The world is waiting, and we're waiting right along with it.

Between my empty stomach, my tired eyes, and the woozy-goo, which is what I'm now calling the stuff Noland covered my face with, I welcome the black out of the things around me. I definitely can't function as my normal self, which is fine by me. Sitting still without the expectation of doing or saying anything is exactly the level of functionality I have right now. Which is good, because there's a lot to consider. By the end of tonight, I'll know if I've excelled to a place Noland has planned for me — for us — or if I'll forever be painting with the desire to reach a higher, more enlightened artistic sense.

And in the silence, no less. The doors haven't opened yet, but I know to listen for the woman's voice who will tell us that everything has started. Wherever a group of Memento Mori members are, The Dignitary is there, waiting to carry us through the next orders.

My head droops down. It wants to drift off, but the echoes of the recorded message keep me from doing so. We are creating a family here, a support network. And it's not just for us. It's for everyone. For all of humanity. Because the world needs to be saved by art.

I straighten back up best I can, putting my head back in place, and patiently wait. It feels like hours, but logic tells me if it had been that long, I would have been knocked out and on the floor— just a welcome mat for everyone to scrape their feet on. Since I'm still sitting — I am still sitting, right? — then it must have been only a few minutes.

Suddenly, I hear something.

Voices. A hoard of them. The door must have opened up and in poured all the voices of Volga county into this building. I try to focus, make sense of what I hear, but even if they are closer than I think, they're still too far away. I stay still, exactly as Noland has instructed. Exactly as the rules were given to me. Eventually, those voices will make their way to where we are, and I'm sure they'll have something to say about the artistic weirdos in masks.

Artistic weirdos. That is how it feels to be a creative mind in a world where hues and shades and brush strokes aren't as valued as bottom line numbers and business structures. Always a weirdo when you have multi colored speckled hands and an unconventional idea at your fingertips.

I'm sure that's what the crowd is murmuring as they browse through the halls and take in all the displayed images chosen for their eyes. Though I hope, I really hope, one or two can at least linger a moment or two longer and truly appreciate what's been given to them.

A piece of ourselves. Each one of us has put a piece of ourselves into our work and the public has the chance to experience that today, if they allow themselves to see it. I imagine a few faceless people standing in front of my wall of art, taking it in, and wondering who the girls are in each of them.

Those who get it will understand. Those who don't, well, I guess they'll just have to be forever lost won't they?

I do wonder, did all my canvases make it? I mean, there were still two Noland asked me to make what now seems like ages ago. Hope they somehow miraculously found their way here. They were brilliant pieces, and if I'm being honest, I'm glad he convinced me to do them. I suppose they must be here, right? If Noland needed them for The Circle, he would have made sure someone would have picked them up, if they did in fact still exist after the fire in the basement.

It's obvious the moment the crowd makes its way to our set up. There are a few gasps, then murmurs. It's difficult to understand what any of them are saying until a man yells, "What a bunch of freaks," clear as day. More murmurs roll out, all in agreement. Weirdos. Creeps. Freaks. Yup, suck it in, banals.

Their disapproval is proof that they were right, the recording, Noland, and every person who stepped foot into the MMS building. Anyone outside of our organization doesn't understand. And you can't support something you don't understand.

Again. I stay still. Even if I had the energy, this isn't the time to fight back. This is the time to allow my canvases to speak for themselves, show that I, too, take my craft seriously. As serious as the plague itself. If these judgemental banals are going to downplay our work, let them. I can't force them to understand my meaning or anyone else's if they're not willing to open themselves up to it.

"Artists are so weird."

"Why are they wearing those creepy masks?"

"And what the heck are they all wearing? That doesn't look right."

"I'll never understand them."

The last voice hits the truth like a nerve. No, these outsiders will never understand. That's why I have to listen to Noland and MMS. They *do* understand. And I. Am. So. Tired. Tired of sitting. Tired of the effort of it. Tired of the circles of conversation I've been having with myself inside my own head. Tired of being tired. A freaking nap would be nice.

I sit. And wait. And hope against hope that within a few moments, someone will close those doors so I can slide to the ground and have a snooze.

But then I hear another voice. One that's silky and smooth. Familiar, like the taste of Joe's coffee first thing in my morning. My stomach complains thinking about it. I will it to stop making noise. Food will come when it's ready. When it's supposed to be ready. I'll eat when they let me know I can. But this voice? That's here and now, and I key into it as much as my foggy brain will allow.

And it only says one thing, "Mills."

Stark. Stark is here.

My heart drops and a painful lump develops in my throat.

Stark is here! And why? Oh my Michaelango, why? Did he see my paintings? Did he hear my message? Did he hear my heart and love of Memento Mori?

I can only imagine his face. His deep eyes drooping, frown lines forming within the dark skin on his forehead. I wonder if his heart feels like mine. If he's missing Livvy like I do. But I can't jump up and hug him. I can't hold him and tell him I miss her, too. I can't say anything to him at all because it would be against the rules.

And I'm far too tired to go against the rules. So I do what I can and tell him I'm okay.

Carefully, with all the energy I have left, I flip my hands over in my lap so my palms face up. I know, this is the bulk of where my soon to be scars are. If Stark is as observant as I believe he is, then he will take notice, smile, and breathe in relief that all is okay.

That's when I hear another voice, even more familiar than Stark's. And that's when I know my brain is turning to mush because it's Livvy.

Livvy who is gone. Livvy who died. Livvy who must be in some other realm because there's no way she's here. I let my palms do the talking. I hope she found a realm that speaks to her just like the realm The Circle speaks to me.

Please let Stark understand my message. I'm okay. I'm fine. I've accepted who I am.

I'm part of the Memento Mori family. And if he can hear this message, then he will be okay, too.

CHAPTER SEVENTEEN

Livvy

"We were so close, Stark! So stinkin' close!" I jam a fist into my palm. Mills was right there within reach and within seconds, she was gone again. And now? Well, what do we have now?

Sucking in a deep breath, I gesture to the wall where Mills's painting is propped up by nothing but hope.

"This isn't enough, Stark. This isn't her." Defeated doesn't even start to cover how I feel.

He runs his hands over his coarse hair. "You're absolutely right. It's not her. Not even close. But, it's a step closer, isn't it?"

"So, what are you going to do with it?"

His little, teensy apartment barely holds him and his three sets of clothing, let alone much more than a loveseat for his sister to sit in. Okay, maybe there's a little more to it. A small dining table, decent sized television. Heck, even his kitchen is a step up from the dorm room I'm used to. Though, it doesn't take much to jump over that low bar.

"I'm keeping it where I can see it every day until she can be here with us. It's a part of her, Liv. And when I get her out of there, I'm going to let her scratch out that imposter's name and put in her own."

"You mean, when *we* get her out." There's no way I'm not a part of this. She was my friend first and I'll do what I can to save her from that sleeze or die trying. Not like I haven't had my brush with death before.

I frown, looking at the canvas, wondering what she was thinking when her brush made those marks. Wondering which brush stroke was her last, before she was swept away to… what exactly? Some linen wearing art cult?

That seems strange. But then again, weirder things have happened.

"Stark, why was she sitting there with them? Lined up with all those other…" I stop myself from calling them freaks, because I know Mills might be eccentric now and then, but she's not a freak. And if she's a part of this group, then there must be something to them that she sees. Or, fears. Or, I don't know.

"Weirdos?" Stark smiles.

I give him a half-smile back. "There has to be a reason why she was there, right? She's not the kind of person to just go along with it for no reason. Do you think she was drugged? Kidnapped? Forced by gun point?"

"Liv, do you remember when we were kids?"

I can't help the way my lips part in a small chuckle. Stark was always into one thing or another. He took apart old toys to repurpose their screws into little robotic arms. He cut up the pages in old books and magazines to create a collage on the inside of his closet doors. Once, he even stripped off the wallpaper in the hallway to see if he could use it for a project. He landed himself a month's worth of extra chores for that one.

"Remember what Mom used to always say?"

I laugh and pull out my best mock-mom voice, "Stark, why are your hands always into everything?"

Stark laughs, too. "She never did understand why I wanted to pull things apart and play with what was left."

"I don't know if any of us really understood it." Absentmindedly, I pick up the remote control nearby and run my fingers over the rubber buttons.

Stark crosses his arms as he sits down in the tiny space next to me. "It wasn't that I wanted to pull things apart. It's that I saw things no one else did. Just like this." He taps the remote on my lap with a finger. "Mom saw I was taking apart the remote control. I saw that each of those buttons could be used to create something textured and cool. I was going to glue them down onto paper and create a pattern based on their size and color. I wanted to know if they felt differently to me if they were put in a different order with a different medium." He shook his head. "Granted, that wasn't one of my best ideas."

I tap the remote, too. "No, it wasn't. Dad made me get up and change the channels for him until you used your allowance money to pay for a new one."

"My point is, Liv, art is weird. It's brilliant and beautiful, and a lot of times it's just plain weird. Most people will look at someone and say, 'that doesn't make any sense' but to the artist themselves, it's all clear. Every bit of clutter, all the little pieces, every detail, it makes perfect sense to the artist who has it in front of them. But unless you're in the artist's head, it's not going to make any sense at all."

Stark rubs his arm and looks up at the ceiling. "And if I'm being honest, sometimes an artist doesn't really know what they're doing either. They just sort of go by their instincts, testing things out, see where it goes. They embrace the process, regardless of what's planned out because the truth is, nothing is ever promised. Sometimes an artist picks up a paper and pencil with the intention to sketch the scenery in front of them, and before they know it, they've created a fictional time warp they forgot they saw in a dream."

He looks back at me, and the confusion I feel must be present on my face. Stark pokes my side. "Hey, how do you think Alice in Wonderland was born?"

I shrug. I always thought it was just a childhood story. Something we used to read together before bed as kids so we'd dream about red roses and rabbits. I never stopped to think about how it was created out of nothing.

"Well, someone once said it was a forgotten dream of Lewis Carrol. He didn't remember it until he sat down to write something. He intended to write one thing, but out came Alice's adventures." He pokes me again. "I don't know how true it is, but I like to think that's the creation story of Alice. Because that's kind of how things sometimes felt when I used to draw or pull things apart for some crazy visual experiment." He pauses for a moment and I can tell he's playing out the last time he picked up a sketch. "Sometimes, I miss it."

I think I get it. Sometimes, artists do things that don't make sense. But as long as they follow their instincts, they're doing what they think is right.

"So yeah." He sighs. "It may not make sense to us as to why Mills is with this group of people. But the fact is, she's there. She told us. And she told us she's okay."

"For now anyway."

"Exactly. The question is," he rubs the bottom of his chin, "who's the artist?"

"Stark, Mills is the artist." Now I'm really not sure I follow him. If he continues down this train of thought, he's going to lose me again right down a rabbit hole.

He walks over to the canvas and traces the brushstrokes with his fingers again. "She's definitely an artist, and a great one at that. But there's someone else who is orchestrating this entire arrangement. And I just can't figure out if it's the woman who seems to think she's better than everyone else or this man here." He taps the signature on the canvas.

"Or both."

"Or both," he echoes. "Some of the most creative pieces are a collaboration."

I join him over at the painting. A collaboration. That makes sense. That last display at the gallery, with all the people in painted masks, that was a collaboration. This painting in front of me with Mills's artwork and Professor Elsinger's signature. That's some kind of collaboration. The entire operation that seems to be operating under an elderly redhead? I suppose that's also a collaboration.

"Stark, this really is sounding like a cult."

"Who better to take on a young impressionable artist who might be feeling a little isolated after being kicked out of college?"

It's true. A freaking cult. Mills has been taken in by a freaking cult. And they're taking advantage of her talent to do what? Claim it as their own? Or something much, much worse.

"How do we get her out? How do we save her before they start feeding her Kool-aide or something?"

"We find where she is."

I nod. "Right. So we just roll up onto Blackwell Avenue, ring the bell, and ask for Mills? Think they'll go for that, Stark? Because I'm pretty sure no cult leader in the history of all cults have ever just allowed anyone out of their grasp without a fight."

"No; you're right. But I have a better idea. We're going in undercover."

The laughter that barks out of me takes me by surprise. "Undercover? Who do you think we are? Sherlock Holmes?"

"Not exactly."

Excitement escapes out of his eyes. He jumps up from his spot and runs — as much as he can run in the tiny apartment — to the bedroom. I have no idea what he keeps back there, and I prefer to keep it that way. But then he comes back into the living room with a pack of shrink wrapped paper.

"Livvy, look at this!" He's excited, nearly bouncing on his heels.

"Stark, it's paper." I don't understand.

"Here." Stark reaches his fingers into the slit of an opening on the plastic wrap and pulls out a single piece of paper. "Smell it."

He hands the sheet of paper to me, and I take it. Just like he asks, I lift it up to my nose and sniff. It's not strong, but it's there. The faint scent of pine.

"Pine, just like the smell at the gallery."

"That's not all, Liv. Remember that address we found?"

"000 Blackwell?"

"Exactly." He flips over the packaging and shows me the message on the back, one of those letters to the customer messages. It says,

Dearest Artist,

We thank you for the purchase of this product. Our paper is made with the utmost care and with the understanding that once in your hands, it has the potential of becoming anything: a gorgeous painting, a page in a sentimental scrapbook, a poetic love letter. The paper you hold in your hand is a blank slate for all the possibilities your imagination can hold. Please, use it wisely. And remember, if you reach the point where you need a safe space to practice your artistic expression with other like minded artists with the freedom to be yourself and stretch your soul, we will be here for that.

"Well, that's a message I didn't expect to see at the back of a ream of paper."

Stark shakes his head and says, "Well, yeah, there's that. But also, look at the bottom."

And there, at the bottom, is the address 000 Blackwell Avenue.

"Huh. That's weird." The exact same address as Professor Elsigner's forwarding address.

"I knew that the address looked familiar, Liv. We sell this paper in the store. Every other week, we get a shipment in, so I see the back of this over and over. It must have just become so routine that it didn't stand out until I forced myself to think about it."

"Okay, so the address of the papermill is the same as the one for Professor Elsigner?"

"And it says right here, this paper could be used to create anything: A painting, scrapbook paper, love letter…"

"…Or a paper mâché mask?"

"Or a paper mâché mask, exactly." Stark plops back down next to me. "It's not traditional paper mâché paper, but it would work. And if that's the case, then it all boils down to this. To paper."

I sit on this for a moment. The paper. The masks. The address. It's all connected. "Stark, you think they'll give us a tour?"

"Sis, that's exactly what I was thinking. We should go find out."

CHAPTER EIGHTEEN

Mills

All ten of us in matching jumpsuits are standing lined up in a room, waiting for our next orders. This isn't a room I've been in before, but it's not completely unlike mine. Well, what used to be mine. Except on the second floor of the building, this one doesn't have any furniture. There's no bed, no table, no sitting chairs or desk. Just a plain room with a bay window looking out on the pine trees in the distance. It's not my room. It just looks very similar. And yet, very different.

The way Noland was talking after the gallery, my room isn't going to be mine anymore. There will be another, and he's assured me it'll be next level. Literally, the next level in the building. Which means, we'll be higher up on the Memento Mori food chain.

Food chain. Food. I force myself to stop thinking about the word.

I force my tongue to stop salivating at the idea of sandwiches.

I force my nose to stop wishing for the scent of stew. Or pork chops. Or banana nut muffins.

I force my stomach to stop asking for more than my own spit to fill it up.

Noland will feed me, when necessary. But for now? Now I need to stand calmly in this room with all the other Memento Mori recruits because we're about to hear the most important news of our lives.

We're about to find out if we're in or out.

The linen outfit I'm dressed in is soft; more comfortable than the clothes I came in here with, all dirty and sweaty from my own grime. These are clean. So clean and so plain, I have to wonder why a group who is so intune with the importance of art itself chose a uniform as blank as a canvas.

Then it hits me. Of course they did. That's the point, isn't it? We're all a blank canvas. It's not until we find our purpose that the canvas gets painted for the world to see, right? And this right here, with the dim lights and the white noise and the waiting for someone to open the doors, this is where we get to find our purpose, right? Or at least get closer to finding it.

My eyes tighten shut, hoping Noland is right, that my canvases were enough, that my paintings were plenty. Of course he's right. He has always been right. He's the one who has taught me every advanced technique and every piece of color theory, and even how to let the art itself speak to me so it just happens on canvas without trying.

And now, he's the one teaching me that there's so much more to loving art than just creating it. It's *being* it. So, yeah, it does make sense why we're all dressed in linen.

A wave of cold air breathes into the room as the doors open. Out come several men without names on their nametags, each wearing their own linen uniform. And each with a jar of paint in their hands. After the men without names comes ten more people. Our handlers, our guides, the people who have believed in us even when we didn't trust who they were.

How silly I was to ever think he would be anything else. When Noland sees me, I fall back into the kindness I knew was always there. His proud smile welcoming me into whatever the next step is. When he comes close, he links his hand in mine and squeezes. I squeeze back. Whatever our past, whatever our misunderstandings, we are in this together, which makes me so grateful I have someone by my side. Someone who understands where my heart is, where it's always been.

Once everyone is in the room, we are all still. Even more silent than we had been before. We wait to see what happens next. I look a few recruits down and see Zak, standing there with Jon behind him. The way his feet dance in place makes me think he's nervous, like he's unsure if what he's done is enough.

A little further down is Paula. We lock eyes for a moment as she gives me a small wave. I get the feeling she's wishing me good luck, like when a friend decides to suck it up and go on a first date with the guy who's been politely asking for months.

Only, this is no first date. This is the rest of my life. Far more important than boys and wishes and fried green tomatoes.

Stop it, brain. We're not thinking about food right now.

I wonder if Paula ever got to see my painting on her hot air balloon. If she ever approved of the locked door that was never really locked. That's what I decided it was, anyway. Because how could it be tightly sealed when it was one of the most freeing images possible? A balloon that can float away anywhere and into nowhere and straight into the Memento Mori where we've become family?

No. I doubt Paula has seen it because I haven't seen what's happened with my machete. What a silly thing to have created in the first place. What did I think I was going to do with that? It's nothing but a loose symbol of how I felt before I understood everything that's currently in front of me right now. And it wasn't up to par. It didn't create the feeling it should have in, well, in anyone else. It just looked like a plain stick.

The Dignitary's voice breaks the silence. "Welcome, artists." Her words are thick and sticky, like she made them that way to linger in our ears. "It is my pleasure to welcome you here today. As you know, our gallery was a success."

For a brief moment, she makes direct eye contact with me, and I swear it's like receiving every congratulatory embrace I've ever worked for. I feel her invisible hug, then she moves on to address the rest of us.

"Recruits, we know you've worked hard to be here. Some of you may have even given your own literal blood, sweat, and gusto in order to be standing here today. Some, without even understanding the full implications of why you've been asked to stand alongside us.

"Recruits, I am so very impressed with what you've come up with. The integrity that lives in your craft is by far some of the best I have seen yet. You should be proud of yourselves for being here, standing alongside the strongest guides within the art world. I know I'm proud of each of you.

"And as for the handlers," her hands lift into the air as she addresses those who are standing next to and behind each recruit. I can feel Noland's excitement radiate through his hand. "You have done well. All of your dedication has not gone unnoticed. And after this, I can promise you, your exploration and purpose will become clearer. Thank you for all you do."

The Dignitary lowers her hands and her smile widens to light up the entire room. "I am so proud of every artistic being in this room. So much, I find it hard for me to contain my energies. But as you know, we must contain ourselves when we have urges that keep us from our higher selves."

"Each and every one of you in this room, in my eyes, is worthy. I wish I could give you each a seat in The Circle. I wish I could override everything Memento Mori has ever taught me and instilled in me and allow you all in." She walks over to Paula and puts her hand on her shoulder. Even from across the room, I can see Paula's confidence move through every piece of her body, straightening up her spine and allowing her eyes to focus where they want. It makes me proud of her, too.

"In fact, if it were up to me, I would say that each one of you would have a reserved seat to the next realm right now." She moves on to the next recruit and touches his shoulder. And the next and the next. When she gets to Zak, he wells up like a proud peacock in heat. I can tell he can hardly wait to show off his next project and the concepts that inspire it. The veins in her petite hand pop a little hello when they squeeze his shoulder.

"But, I'm afraid it's not up to me."

The energy in the entire room shifts. It's like a hand has a hold on the atmosphere and is squeezing it the same way the frail lady in front of me is squeezing everyone's shoulders.

She moves on, now only a few stops away from me. "I know each of you are brilliant. And many of you understand that we aren't alone in all of this. There is a driving force who leads and educates us, guiding us in each necessary movement. But for those of you who don't know—" Her hand reaches my shoulder. When it squeezes, I can feel warmth radiate through me in prickles of excitement and nerves. "The deity that speaks to us has a name. It's Dali da Monet."

Like Salvador Dali. Leonardo DaVinci. And Monet. Former me would say that's too obvious. Today me understands how mystically imperative it all is, hearing the words of the classical artists in today's world. Of course that's who guides us. Of course that's who gets to decide whose expression is more worthy than others.

As she leaves my side to again address the entire room, I can still feel her touch linger under the linen on my shoulder. "And They have spoken to me. After seeing what you brought to our gallery, the collective voice has come to me and She has told me exactly who has a seat in The Circle to approach the next realm."

She sucks in her breath, and as she lets it out, everyone in the room is waiting on their own breath to hear what she has to say next. "They have told me those names, but I want to assure everyone in this room that you all hold an importance. Even if you're not selected, even if your name isn't written in the stars to leave what we currently know as reality right now, I don't want you to feel discouraged. See, the fact that you're here, ready and willing to explore your artistic expression, is proof that your importance does not end here. In fact, it's just starting. Our family still needs you, regardless of where Dali da Monet has placed your name."

The Dignitary, I wish I could recall her actual name, takes three backward steps to the door, allowing room for the men without names to step forward with their jars of paint. I watch each of them twist open their jars, though they're all tilting the tops in a way that hides the colors inside.

I drop Noland's hand I had been holding the entire time, though I haven't been paying attention to it at all. Whether it was there or not doesn't make any difference. I grab hold of my linen clothes and feel their smooth texture run through my fingers. It won't be long before we're no longer blank canvases. Soon, we'll see what message will be given to us to carry. Will we be pegged as worthy of the next realm? The Circle? Or something completely unknown?

I close my eyes to fight back my excitement and trepidation. I don't want to squeal out of place, ruining the entire mood of the room.

"Ladies and gentlemen, your futures."

I can feel those words fill me up as if an entire unearthly force is behind them. But before I can wonder if it has something to do with Dali da Monet, I feel it. Wet, sticky splotches hit my arms and legs. A large puddle forms on my chest and one splatter whacks against my cheek. A jelly-like trail drips down my neck and runs all the way to my clavicle.

Cheers erupt around me, and I open my eyes. Half the room is coated in reds. The other half, blues. Everyone around me is jumping up and down in delight. Even Paula is making little hops, red paint dripping off her linens. I suppose the excitement is so contagious, not even she can keep from experiencing it.

Swinging my head to the side, I see Noland. He also has red paint splattered on his clothes. A little has landed on his upper lip, so when he smiles, it traces within his laugh lines. Now, I can't help it and we're both laughing giddily. My toes are bouncing up and down off the floor in rapid movements, and everything feels so light. The sea of blues and reds around me moves in waves, and for a brief moment, I can't even see the separation between them.

They're all purple.

We're all purple.

We're all the same, we're all aspiring artists under the same roof, dancing around a leader with multiple colors on her clothes.

A single, slow clap stops our celebration. Every voice quietens. All the jumping stops. And just as quickly as it all blurred, it's separated again. We're blue. Or red. Not the mixture. Not the same. Totally different from The Dignitary's garb.

The Dignitary pulls her hands apart and says, "Good."

Good. Okay. Good what?

And as if she can read my mind, she answers, "Good. I'm so glad to see the excitement erupt in this room. As you can see, you have now been marked into two groups. From this moment on, Handlers and recruits, you'll be staying in your own group. You'll be working together while honing your crafts separately. You'll be expressing yourselves as a collective of red or a collective of blue."

With that, she leaves. She just up and leaves the room as if that answers everything. Or anything. What do the colors mean?

I see the worried look on Paula's face, too, but her eyes look up into mine and I give her a reassured smile. We're good. We're really good. And I saw the intricacies she created in her paper mâché. With her construction and my painting, I have all the confidence that she and I and everyone else with red splotches all over them are in. We're in. We're moving on. Noland will be in The Circle and so will Paula's handler. Paula and I will have spaces in the next realm. We made it. And we will feel it. We'll get to know the pleasure of absolute euphoria. Where all people are no longer people, but we're souls who understand the importance of expression and art and the messages it creates.

Two men without names separate from the crowd and stand by a door on either side of the room. The five who have hands covered in blue paint collect on one side of the room. The five with red collect on the other. That's our cue. We take the hint and instinctually separate in our new color-coded crowds.

Paula stands next to me, and I can't help it. I wrap my arms around her and pull her close. "We made it," I say with my embrace. "We made it," I say with my words.

But when I look up from our hug, something catches my eyes across the room. That's when I realize Zak didn't make it. He's in the blue group, and he's being taken away. I feel like I'm losing a brother. He won't get to know euphoria. He won't get to free his soul. He won't hear Dali da Monet's voice and feel Their guidance.

Zak gives me a fleeting look as his group leaves out the opposite side of the room, and I feel the shuffling of my group — the red group — push me out the other. No time to feel sorry for Zak and the others. We're on our way to freeing our souls.

CHAPTER NINETEEN

Noland

Red paint drips down my forehead. It rides the side of my nose. I can feel it creep into the stinging corners of my eyes, and I can taste it on my mouth. It's sweeter than you'd think. I'm covered in it from head to toe with splashes and splatters, and I've never been happier.

Just moments ago, I was holding onto the hand of the most important person in this life. The person who got me here in this seat, in The Circle. Everything I have ever needed.

Just moments ago, I felt her warmth run through me, beating within my heart and running the same veiny highways as the blood that keeps me alive. But it feels like ages ago since that electricity filled me. Now, walking single file with the other handlers and their recruits, the new Circle members, I feel miles away from the one person I want to stand next to. From the warmth I want to hold onto. I should thank her for staying near me later.

For now, one of the No Names is walking us upstairs to the third story of the building. And if I'm honest, it looks nothing like I thought it would. I figured it would be another carbon copy of the first two floors I've had access to before. The same rooms lining the halls of a large circle, mostly singular accommodations for each recruit and handler pair with a few community rooms for instruction, meditation, and artistic discoveries.

The No Name scans a card to allow us through the locked door. And now we're here, I see exactly why those who earned this spot are called The Circle. This floor is a circle. Okay, I know that I said the other floors were circular, too, but this one feels different. It feels bigger. It feels like there's so much more to offer here. Only, we have access to half of it. On this end, there's another locked door, blocking us from access to whatever is behind it. It would only make sense there's another locked door halfway around, keeping us contained. Contained to half a circle.

That's okay. It doesn't matter. We're still there. We're still in it. We've still made it. We are still The Circle, regardless of semantics.

And looking at the blonde standing a foot in front of me, I am so proud of how far we've come, together. So proud that she's by my side. Not technically, but she definitely got me here, even if I did have to bend a few rules to do it. Sometimes we're meant to shapeshift around the rules a little to do what's necessary. Especially when it involves the realm of enlightenment.

Now that everyone is on the floor, the No Name stops us from moving any further. He holds his hands up, still stained in red paint.

"Before we move further, I've been ordered to give you all this." He shoves a hand into a pocket and pulls out a stack of cards, just like the one that allowed us to get to this level. He reaches back into his pocket and pulls out a set of wristbands, red, just like the paint we're coated with. "Each of you gets a key card randomly assigned to a number. This will allow you into this floor and in the designated area. No further. It will also allow you into your assigned room. You will not have access to anyone else's personal space. Your individual rooms are built so you can have the rest, relaxation, and tools you need to explore whatever creativity may spark your interest. In fact, I'm sure you'll find there are some new supplies you'll want to delve into. For the handlers, as always, you're allowed on all the grounds outside of this building. Recruits, consider yourselves free to travel the grounds as well. Other buildings are still off-limits unless you ask for explicit permission from The Dignitary herself. Please keep your key card safe as you only get one."

At the sound of rest and relaxation, the crowd lets out a collective sigh. That is, everyone but me and Mills. I do my best to echo the sound to give the impression that I, too, did my duties to the fullest. Telepathically, I try to tell Mills to do the same.

He hands out the key cards, one to each person in red stained linen. Each person he hands a card to also holds out their wrist for a red wristband. When Mills gets hers, I note the number on it. Seven. She's staying in room seven. My heart sinks when I get a glimpse at my own room number. Two. I'm all the way on the other side of the half-circle. I've been by her side this entire time and now I'm being ripped away by five digits.

She follows the steps of the person before her, some girl who I thought from day one never had it in her. She's been shy and coy and her hands have only created mediocre pieces. But she's here, too. So I suppose The Dignitary and Dali da Monet saw something in her that my meager eyes don't see. I'm taking note on that. She's one to watch.

"When you reach your room number, please help yourself inside. You should have everything you need behind the door, including some gifts from The Dignitary." The No Name points his hands to the first door with a large black number one hanging on it.

One of the handlers, a woman with jet-black hair, quietly helps herself to the door. She scans her card and lets herself in. For the brief moment her door is open, I see a single table laden with little cardboard boxes with black and white printed labels. But she closes the door before I can read any of them.

Not that it matters. We shuffle along a couple of feet and we meet the door with a number two on the front. My door. I grimace. My stop on this train has come way too early on this journey. And my Mills, my muse, my Emily, is still trudging forward. Her journey is longer, and I wish I could continue to be part of it.

The card in my hand feels cold, untouched and unloved by anyone else. I take that feeling as comfort that whatever I am about to walk into has my name written all over it. Whatever it is, is untouched by anyone else, too. As the rest of the line marches forward and away, I place my card in the slot, matching the number two on the card to the two above the handle.

Like magic, it opens. I can almost hear my name being whispered in the hiss of the door. "Noland," it says, and I can feel it in my bones. This is mine. My new home meant just for me.

The rooms two floors below are a joke compared to this. They may have felt like a getaway at a three star hotel, but this is more like a fully furnished five star apartment. The first thing I see is the same table I got a glimpse of, with similar boxes laid out in a neat row. I'll get to those later.

First, I want to see what's behind the door on the far wall. I pass up a tiny kitchenette, with an open area bar. I pass another door, this one open and clearly a bathroom. Standard. Similar to the old one I'm used to. But it's bigger with an extra large tub with what looks like jets inside. For warm baths instead of cleansing ones. That will be nice. But that's not what I'm most excited about. The door that's closed in front of me holds secrets I want to know.

When I reach it, I put my hand on the handle. A light push down and it opens. What greets me feels like a welcome home I never knew I needed. The king sized bed towers over the twin that lived downstairs. Its pillowy comforter already feels like a hug, and I haven't even touched it. But that's just the start. This bedroom is huge. Large enough to hold an oversized recliner in the corner, a side table next to both it and the bed, an ottoman my feet can't wait to test out, and a dresser. A whole dresser built out of pine, and with six large drawers.

I can't imagine anything being inside those drawers, but I grab the handles with both hands and pull. The pine scent erupts into the air, and inside I find a stack of new clothes. All linen. All in my size. All freshly pressed and folded. Just. For. Me.

This is a relief. Even though I've only worn my set of linen for a few days in a row, I haven't washed them in weeks. Not since The Dignitary gave them to me. They've only aired out on days when I was scanning the banal world for a recruit. But when recruiting time was over and I had to drop the old world for the real one, this was all I had. And now, I'm gifted new clothes. Fresh ones, for a fresh start.

I tear off my dirty linens and let them fall to a lump on the floor. For a moment, I let my bare body enjoy a breeze without any fabric sticking to it. It tingles across my skin and makes everything under my underwear feel fresher than it has in days. Feeling the air conditioning hit my skin like this is a cleanse of its own. Shedding the first floor me and stepping into the new me. Perfection.

Patience, I remind myself. Patience. Everything is requiring a lot of patience for all the stars to align and make this all right. My mouth sucks in a breath and I hold it within my lungs and let my body dangle for another minute before pulling out a fresh new pair of linens to slip into. Somehow they're both crisp and loose, the perfect texture to tell me no other body has ever climbed into them before. They're virgin pants, and that electrifies me.

The shirt slips over just as easy. The sleeves hang off my arms like a comfortable cling film that keeps coming back for more. The hood hangs behind my neck. It's a clean hug waiting to grasp hold at the back of my head, but I let it dangle there. It can stay waiting patiently, just like I am.

Now fully clothed, I leave the reddened pile of clothes on the floor and place my hand on the bedroom door to leave. I love this room. Everything about it speaks volumes as to how valuable The Dignitary really believes I am. How valuable we all are.

Well, everyone except those who left the initiation ceremony wearing blue.

My knuckles rap on the door, leaving any thought of the artists in blue behind. I shouldn't be thinking about them at all, no matter how much potential Jon or the recruit of his might have had. I may have even liked the both of them, if given a little more time. I shouldn't be thinking of them. I should be thinking about what my next steps are and how to treat them to treat myself.

Goodbye blue artists. See you in the next realm when Dali da Monet believes you're ready.

I pass the kitchenette on the way back. I don't need to go through the cabinets to know what's in them. Guarantee it's very similar to before. Paint jars for when artistic inspiration strikes and medicinal bottles with Doctor James's signature attached to them. Though, there are more cabinets and drawers in the back. Maybe I will take a look as to what's in them a little later.

But first, the table.

Resting on the tabletop are a handful of cardboard boxes, each with little labels. This is what I'm now most interested to find out about. I want to know what gifts are inside those cardboard walls.

The one closest to me is small, but I don't even need to read the label to know what's inside. The jingling that sounds off when I pick it up is enough to tip me off. Handheld pottery tools to make little cuts and grooves into soft material. Nice.

The next box is slightly larger. This one I do read. Scraping tools, it says. Perfect for texturizing clays and dough. Each one inside has a different handle, so if one grip doesn't feel right in my hand, then another will. I pull out one with a flat handle and a jagged edge. It's like a comb, but more rounded in shape and with teeth that could hurt.

Out of curiosity, I drag it across my forearm and watch it prick my skin with wonder. It feels a little like a row of papercuts. Only, not nearly as bad. I can handle it. Curiosity will be my painkillers. Within seconds, crimson droplets appear on top of my skin. The loose, yet clingy, sleeve hugs onto my arm for a minute before it gives up its grip again. My clothes are no longer virgin clothes. They're coated in blood and match the same shade of red as the clothes that are now at the bottom of my bedroom.

It's actually fascinating the way my skin is now textured in stripes, like my doughy skin itself is living clay. I scan the other boxes on the table. Maybe clay is in one of these. Dotting tools. Carvers. Sponges. Pallet knives. No clay. My hands sift through each one, just in case whoever labeled them missed it. My fingers feel all textures, cold metal, drab plastic, and little rounded pieces and several serrated edges. But anything resembling the soft, squishy wetness of clay is missing.

Just then, I hear a distant knock. I go to answer it, but when the door opens, no one is there. I take a single step out and realize the knock wasn't at door number two. It was at number one. There, the lady with long dark hair is at her door and her guest is none other than Doctor James.

"For you." Doctor James hands her a small bottle. When he jiggles it a little, I hear a single *tik tik tik* inside.

She takes the bottle from his hand and jingles it, too. *Tik tik tik.* Without saying anything, she questions him with a look.

"It's for The Circle. It's for enlightenment," he says.

And then that's it. That's the entire conversation. She closes the door and he walks away. I expect for him to stop by my room, too, so I stand by, stand guard. I wait right in the doorway.

"Hey, Noland." He waves to me.

I return the favor. "Good day, Doctor James."

And then he leaves. He doesn't hand me any bottle. He doesn't tell me what was in the one he gave to Door Number One. He doesn't say anything about The Circle. He just leaves.

I won't admit that I'm jealous. I just slink back into room number two, wondering why I don't get the special treatment Room Number One gets.

I sit down at the table and go back to the scrapers. My linens are already stained, so I might as well play with the different tools given to me. See what else they can provide me. See if exploring them will get me closer to the enlightenment I need.

CHAPTER TWENTY

Mills

It turns out, there are several large pine trees planted on the grounds. More than I had seen from the window of the room that was mine and now not. And my new favorite place has become sitting under one of them. I just decided. Just now. I guess the permission to leave the walls of the building in front of me is exactly what I needed to find a place that feels a little like home. Feeling the freshly cut grass underneath my hands, the sun's warmth kissing my cheeks, and the slightest breeze that reaches all the way through my clothes.

Yes, I realize how cliché that all sounds. Today, I'm fine being a cliché. I hope all days I can be a cliché. As happy as a clam, with a new lease on life, as luck would have it. Yadda yadda yadda. Just pile up all the hackneyed phrases of happiness right on my lap. I'll take them.

My gaze gravitates to the building in front of me with a strange smokey haze behind it. I wonder which of the windows was mine on the first floor? I'm not entirely sure. All I have to go on is a pine tree stump, and well, there are quite a few of those on the grounds, too.

But you know what I can see? My room. My real room. Seventh room down on the third floor.

I smile, grateful for everything inside. A fresh set of clothes was exactly what my skin needed. New art supplies was exactly what my heart needed. And the chicken nuggets that were waiting for me in the freezer? Well, I could barely finish their minute and a half in the microwave before I shoved that little dino-shaped deliciousness down my throat.

They were even more delightful than I last remember.

And now, with a full tummy and a view even Edward Hopper would be jealous of, I feel like I've wiped my canvas clean again. I'm ready to start over, yet again. Ready to take on the world with whatever new creative challenge comes my way, including the concept of the realm above reality.

I frown. It's hard being utterly happy for yourself, knowing you've made it to a level of respect and admiration, and at the same time knowing half of the people who were gunning for the position weren't going to make it there. Zak and all the other blue people. What will happen to them?

It shouldn't matter. The Dignitary told us that those who didn't make it into The Circle would still have purpose, right? So even if Zak didn't make it to the right side of things, he'll still be here. He'll still have a place in MMS where his talent will be used. Ha, looks like maybe he's the one who didn't craft up to par after all. I bet he's eating his words right now.

"Emily Ellis." The familiar voice calls me out of my thoughts. The Dignitary is standing above me, looking down at my seat by the tree. Instantly, I move myself off the ground and into a standing position. With flailing fingers, I dust off my pants. Dirt flies off, but the freshly mowed grass left a stain that won't come off with any brushing. At least I'm not still sitting on the ground. It feels disrespectful addressing someone of such high stature from the view of the dirt.

"Hello, Dignitary." I give her my best smile, hoping it'll cover up the imperfections on my newly gifted clothes.

"Please, call me Iris."

So, her name is Iris. Like the Iris who signed my note. I don't know why, but knowing that makes the mysticality of Memento Mori sort of evaporate. Maybe there was no mystery at all. Maybe all it took was a little willingness to understand this operation to see through it and get to the humanity behind everything.

I try out her name, "Alright, hello, Iris." It feels like a foreign object in my mouth.

"How are you enjoying your time out here in the open?"

I give her a nod and breathe in the fresh air. "It's nice." It's better than nice.

"I thought you might like it, Emily. And I thought you might like this, too."

My eyes draw to her hands in front of her. She's holding a box, very similar to the boxes that greeted me in my room. Only this one is labeled with a word that was missing on all the others: Clay.

My heart leaps into my throat. I failed the paper mâché test. I redeemed myself in painting. But that was obvious. Painting is my medium of choice. Clay is going to give me the chance to show I can do whatever the hell is thrown at me. I can do more than brush strokes and color theory.

With a little lump of clay, I could put any one of those tools to play and create anything at all. Anything. This is the moment I live for as an artist, where nothing has yet been created, but I know with a little bit of time, my materials will find their voice and something magical will materialize. And this time, I get to prove my worth by expanding my talents even more.

"Is that for… me?" Even though she offered it up, it feels too big for me to assume. And I don't want to make an ass out of…well, you know what assume spells.

She nods, and even through her thick lenses, I can see her eyes sparkle.

As she extends her arms out, I can see the little lump inside, cut into a perfect square and wrapped in plastic. Virgin clay that's never been touched by anyone else's hands. It electrifies me.

"Thank you," I say, and when I take the box, it feels like I'm taking a piece of treasure only I know how to appraise.

"Be good to it," she tells me. "Use it as practice. Find which tools speak to you the most. Knowing which ones feel best to you is going to be so valuable when the time comes."

When the time comes. That's been a big question lurking in the back of my gut. The enlightenment. The ascension. The next realm. We're all reaching to the next level, but how much longer until we get to the ultimate goal?

"When is that, Iris?" Her name still feels like it wants to stick between my teeth. "When will the time be?"

She gives a little gravely chuckle. "Don't you worry your little head about that, Emily. The time will come soon enough. Your time, even sooner." She blows me a kiss and walks away. Somehow, that doesn't even seem strange here. I almost want to throw my palm up in the air and catch the invisible smooch and keep it close to my heart.

I don't. I contain myself.

But now I have a box of clay. I poke at it with a finger. Underneath the plastic, I can still feel its soft outside give a little while the hardened interior keeps its shape. All it will take is a little manipulation for it to be something completely different, exciting, a new living, breathing organism. Or as close to a living breathing organism as this fleshy-colored clay can be.

Guess it's time to take it back to the room and play with it like Iris said. Poke it and prod it, scrape its outsides and texturize what I can see so I can morph it into what I can't.

My time is coming soon, like she said.

CHAPTER TWENTY-ONE

Livvy

A swig of warm tea coats the inside of my mouth. Warm and sticky, it's exactly the right thing to calm my beating heart. Especially from the passenger's seat. Of a car that's seen better days. While Stark is speeding down the road. Maybe beating heart isn't how I should phrase it. Thrashing might be more accurate.

Every turn feels like a personal whiplash, and each time it jolts the atoms in my body alive.

"You know where you're going?" I ask with tightened eyes. I'm afraid if I open them, my stress will multiply enough to force my heart to leap straight out of my ribcage, and out into the open. Then I'll have to worry about my own health when I need to focus on Mills's.

"Just a few miles down this next dirt road and we'll find Blackwell Avenue."

I don't know why I even asked. Everyone knows where Blackwell is. Everyone has been by its gates and looked inside. It's just that not everyone knows how to get past them or knows what's behind the limited view from the gate entrance.

We turn again, my entire body snapping left, my arm forced to brush up against Stark's. He's a little gross-sweaty, but I suppose I probably am, too. Anxiety will do that to a person. Little rumbles shake the car and my eyes are forced to open. Part of me expects to see the trunks of trees in front of me, the entire car skidding off the road.

But we're not. Stark's turned down on a gravel road. I guess when he said dirt, he meant gravel. There's a big difference, especially when it comes to how a car may handle speed on it. But I'm not about to correct him. Not with the determined look he's giving the space in front of us.

So I keep my mouth shut and let the rumble underneath us reassure me that we're only moments away.

"Woo-sahh," I let out in the open.

Moments away from what, though, that's what I'm not so sure about. What are we going to do when we get there? Knock on the gates and ask nicely to be let in? Tell whoever answers we just need to get in quickly to retrieve our friend and peace out?

There is no way it's going to be that easy.

"What did you find?" Stark's words seep out of his gritted teeth.

I swallow back my instant response. I agreed to do some research, find out whatever I could about pine trees and paper. It's the only thing we really have and any kind of knowledge I might get from it could be an advantage. But my research didn't show up much. I don't want to tell him "nothing important." Even if it feels like it might not be, all research is deathly important. So, I spill it out.

"Well, I found that most paper is made from pine trees."

"So there's nothing special about our paper?" He sounds annoyed, but I know it's not at me. It's at our momentary situation. His brain wants answers and my brain has yet to give them.

"Not in the make of it, necessarily. But I could smell a little pine on it when you handed me a piece, and that's not normal. Most paper doesn't smell like the tree it comes from."

"So what does that mean?"

I hold back a shrug, because I really don't know what it means, but I don't want to add onto the discouragement we both feel at the moment.

"It means there's something else in that paper."

The quiet between us is loud. I let it fill up the car as we travel along this road a little longer, and I search in my memory for something else that might be useful. I can't come up with anything substantial, so my mind acts out for me. It starts to recall everything I've ever known about pine trees and the products that come from them. And, well, my mouth decides to go ahead and spout off those recalls out loud without a second thought.

"Well, some people make things out of pine. Arts and crafts type stuff like wax and candles and air fresheners. Maybe the paper mill does that kind of thing, too? Maybe they add a little pine-scented potpourri that lingers on the paper?" I know I'm reaching for connections.

"Maybe," he says. Then he repeats himself in an even quieter voice, "Maybe." It sounds like he's losing hope on figuring out more the closer we get to our destination.

The car continues forward for a little until there's one more jolting turn. Then, Stark stops. There is nowhere else to move forward to. Right in front of us is a giant iron gate, closed, and I assume locked. All the Volga folklore floods my memories. A family that locks themselves away never to be seen again. No matter who rattles the gates, no one comes forward. The scenery and whoever is behind it is left to overgrow and become forgotten.

The words continue to find their way out of me. I suppose my sensory apparatus is coping the best way it can. "Of course, there are people who use pine trees medicinally, too." My nerves shake the words out without my mind able to damn my mouth shut. "Tea from needle buds for coughs, or boiled down needles as a diuretic."

Stark is already out of the car. Following his lead, I open my own door and step out, too.

"Fresh pine needles and cinnamon for sinus relief. To drink, though. Not to shove up there. That would probably burn. And even as a drink, I imagine it's an acquired taste, being so pungent and sticky." The strong scent of pine around us invades my nose so strong, I can taste it. Even the smell is sticky, attaching itself to the tiny hairs inside my nose and refusing to let go.

"The Chinese use the bark in wine, which I gotta say is pretty intriguing. It's probably an acquired taste, too. I wonder what the alcohol content is in it and if anyone on campus would swap out their bottom shelf beers with something so adventurous." I suck in a breath before I trip over each individual thought. "But other people throw some in their bath to soak in after a long day of work. Since the resin is a historic antimicrobial wash, I imagine it might actually do well with muscle pain. Probably good for manual labor type people. Maybe you should consider it yourself after a workout." If he hears my suggestion, he doesn't respond to it. This isn't the time nor space to strike up a conversation about his exercise routine.

Stark's hand touches the metal gate, and I can feel the beat of my heart accelerate to an even more abnormal pace. I didn't even know that was safely possible. My thoughts keep spilling out of my mouth, and I hope it's enough to slow down any tachycardia.

"In fact, pine is known as the forest's natural bandages. So if you're ever stuck out in the woods with an open wound and without a first aid kit, you can just grab a little pine bark and slap it on there. It'll clear it up nicely, even better than typical topical solutions."

Cling. Cling. Cling. The metal rings out to the same rhythm of Stark's shaking.

"And if you're crafty enough, you can make your own dimethyl sulfoxide. But I don't know why anyone would make it when you can just grab a bottle of it on any pharmacy shelf. DMSO is pretty cool stuff, though. It's like nature's aspirin. Rub it wherever you need and inflammation goes down. Perfect to cure up any cut or scrape or blemish."

When Stark's hands release their grip from the metal bars in front of us, he scans the rest of the gate to come up with a plan B. He does. It's a call box with a single button on it. I'm not sure why I didn't notice it before or why the town rumors seem to conveniently leave it out. I guess scary stories don't include a simple way to contact the people you're wanting answers from. A loud *beep* sounds when he presses it. Part of me hopes no one answers. Part of me knows if no one does, we're back to square one.

"And what's really awesome about DMSO is that it can actually make you feel better quicker if you have an open wound. Totally numbs the pain and everything so you can heal up a whole lot faster. Maybe I should actually grab some to keep in a first aid kit."

"Can I help you?" a voice rings from the call box. It doesn't sound annoyed or angry. It's not mysterious and creepy. It's not even questioning us in a way I expect anyone to question intruders. But I guess we aren't exactly intruding, are we?

"Completely numb, Stark. Not even my extra-strength aspirin can do that."

Stark lifts a finger up to his mouth to shush me, and I suck in my nervous lip so I can bite any more instantaneous thoughts back.

"Hello, yes. We are here to talk to someone about your paper manufacturing?" Stark has always been great at perfecting his nice customer salesman voice. "We're from one of your distributors, Craft Your Pants crafting supply store. We're interested in carrying more of your products in stock and wanted to talk to someone about the available options."

When the voice doesn't respond back, Stark clears his throat and tries again. "We apologize for arriving unannounced. We would have called, except we couldn't find any phone number on file. Definitely a hiccup on our end. All we had to go on is an address. Just ten minutes, please. Our customers have been asking for more locally sourced supplies, and we know you would be a great fit for our needs."

That's all it takes for the call box to click, buzz, and allow the gate to unlatch itself and swing open. A path lined out in front of us tells us where we should go. A sign right off the path tells us the car isn't allowed on their perfectly manicured lawn. My teeth let go of my lip, and as we take a step through, I can't help myself to continue on with the thoughts I had paused.

"Shouldn't everyone have something that magical, Stark? Some handy DMSO you can just put on anything and never feel its pain? A cut? A scrape?" Then, it hits me. "A burn?" The word leaks out in a whisper.

"Stark!" I grab his arm and grip it with every molecule I have. "Stark, what if that's it?"

Maybe it's because he hasn't been able to catch up with my scattered thoughts. Or maybe it's because he's been making move after move with his own strategy. But his dark eyes read confusion. "What do you mean, Liv?"

"Think about it. If they're using pine trees to make paper, there will be a lot of extra byproducts left over. One of those byproducts *is* DMSO, Stark. And on the shelf, it smells a bit like garlic, but what if it's not something that's on the shelf? What if it doesn't go through the extra steps to purify it before it's used? They wouldn't have to if they're not selling it for commercial use. And if it's not completely purified, it might just smell a little like its original essence."

"So you think the paper we sell in the store has some kind of… liquid aspirin that smells like pine? Livvy, that sounds like a stretch."

"Here me out, Stark. Maybe they don't purposefully slather their sheets, but maybe it's just something that happens. Kind of like a work hazard that's just expected when you're doing so much. Maybe the scent itself is some kind of byproduct they don't really consider getting rid of. It doesn't really matter, though. What matters is off of the paper."

"Meaning?"

We take a few more steps before I continue on. I want to make sure I get the next part right, clear. I know my brain is pinging around like crazy cakes.

"Meaning, what if the reason why Mills was sitting at the gallery as calm and collected as she was is because she was numb? What if Professor Elsinger or whoever has her under control put some kind of DMSO solution on her burn wounds and it sort of… knocked her out? If it's a concentrated byproduct, even if it's mixed with something, it may actually be a lot stronger than off-the-shelf stuff. Scarily strong."

"Well then, I guess that answers one thing."

"She's definitely not here of her own free will."

"Maybe she wasn't telling us she's okay after all."

CHAPTER TWENTY-TWO

Livvy

"Hello, my friends."

This man in front of us came out of nowhere. If Mills were here, she'd probably say he popped into existence like a ghostly Jack-in-the-box wearing a jumpsuit. And if you ask me, no one wears linen jumpsuits for fun, so this guy either never changed out of his garb from the gallery or the entire cult thing is getting very, very real.

I remind myself, Mills is here. She has to be here, and it's our job to find her. So if this Jack-in-the-box-in-a-linen-jumpsuit considers us friends, then we are friends, regardless of how insane this scenario feels. It's another step closer to finding her.

"Hello." I wave to him.

Stark juts out a hand. I guess he's still in business-man mode, and I need to quietly follow his lead the best I can. Which means, staying quiet and following their footsteps.

"It's nice to meet you…" His voice dangles, hoping to get a name out of this man.

But the man in front of us just nods and smiles. Then he says, "Come this way."

I try to read off his name tag, to give me something, but there's nothing there. It's blank. Perhaps an oversight of whoever his boss is. Speaking of oversight, this actually does seem a little too easy. We really did just press a button and ask for entry. Now we're here, I don't know if I should be thankful for the ease or concerned over whatever the illusion might be covering up.

We follow him, just a few feet behind his steps, and I do my best to record every detail of our surroundings. It's almost like we're on campus, only there are a few details that make it feel off. The field-like grass is *too* meticulously cut. Each building is outlined with *too many* azaleas and daisies. There are several little walking highways weaving in and out of the buildings, each a little *too* precise in their direction, and each building shines a little *too* brightly in the sunline to be nearly reflective. It's all a little too perfectly kept, like hiding behind a locked iron gate isn't enough. Nor is it enough to hide behind a line of thick pine trees bordering the property. It also has to hide behind a mask of perfection.

A lifetime of experiments and tests and research has told me nothing can possibly be perfect. There are always variables to throw off the observer. The missing name on the man's name tag is one, but I bet the more we climb inside this place, the more variables I'll find.

We all step to the side as a little motorized cart drives up to us. Another man in the same linen jumpsuit is behind the wheel. He gives a small, listless wave and drives by. It's the only interaction we get on our little walk. The only sign of life outside the three of us. After that, it's back to keeping in perfect step on our little journey to who knows where.

To the left is a large circular building with a foggy sky behind it.

No. Not foggy. Smoggy.

Each floor is lined with oversized bay windows. Hanging baskets with green leaves spilling over in all directions dot the middle of each one. Those are definitely not office spaces. They look more like fancy cookie-cutter accommodating apartments. More carbon copies of perfection that don't feel quite right.

"This way, please," the man in front of us veers right, and I do my best to give Stark an eye-full of my thoughts. They're holding people in that building. Mills is probably one of them, each being indoctrinated to believe… well, I don't know what they're being told to believe.

We continue to follow our guide's steps, walking past several stand alone pine trees along the way. I notice a girl sitting on a fresh stump, sawdust still sprinkled around the edges. Her short strawberry-red hair covers her face, dangling over her eyes as she bends her gaze toward the ground. At first glance, I think she's crying. I want to run to her, hug her, shake her, and ask if she's seen Mills. See what variable she holds. But then I realize she has something in her hand. It's a ball of red clay, staining her hands as she kneads it. I've seen this before. She's not crying. She's intent like a good artist should be. Like all the great artists already are.

Just as I start to wonder if that's the entire point of this place, to provide an artistic space because that is what would make sense, I notice something else. Two more people are standing by a bench, each of them with clay-colored hands. They hand their pieces back and forth as if the only way to achieve what they both want is for the two of them to each have their hands in the creation of it.

Behind them is an open field. Or, what would be an open field if it didn't have five large supportive pedestals. On top of each is a small item. Some have multiple. But they don't seem to have any connection to each other. At first, it seems like they're all animals: A lion head, an elephant, and giraffe are pretty easy to spot. But then I see a guitar, which isn't even painted in animal print. It throws me off when I get to a fluorescent cactus and several oddly shaped blobs of color. Stark is right. Sometimes art is weird.

There's a single empty pedestal. I wonder what's supposed to be on there. Or what might have been taken from it. And then I see a miniature hot air balloon I wish I could hop into and take a ride because the brushstrokes on it look so familiar. I grab hold of Stark's arm and squeeze. "Look," I whisper-yell and point over into the direction of the display. "That's hers." I force my words to be so quiet, they can only reach Stark. "That has to be hers."

Under my grip, I can feel his muscles contract. He sees it, too. He knows it, too. The question is, where is she now?

A few more feet and I pull my eyes away from the hot air balloon and all the other displayed projects. A giant factory with big, billowy smoke plumes draws my attention away from them. That's what the smog is from. That's what was clouding the sky.

I'm somewhere between wanting to run straight through its front doors and wanting to run straight in the opposite direction. This leaves me and the men next to me dragging on at a painful pace. Left step. Right step. Left step. It's all the mechanics of walking from here.

"So how many trees does the paper mill process each month?" I don't have any real reason to ask. I just need to break up the left, right, left pattern that's driving me insane. "With the amount of paper you produce, I imagine you're making a dent into the forest that surrounds your…" I struggle to find a term for the area we're in. Grounds? Campus? Square?

"Commune," he says. "And you'd be surprised. A single pine tree can produce over 800 pounds. And that's just the paper."

Stark jabs in me in my side.

"Just the paper?" I ask. And then I bite my lip to keep any more questions from spilling out. I don't want to get off track before he answers this question.

"Waste not want not. Isn't that the expression?"

"So, what other products come out of your warehouse?" Stark is doing his best to keep his salesman's face on while picking through any clues we notice. "I'm sure our customers might be interested in what else we could store on our shelves for their use."

Before we hear any answer, we reach the entrance. Our unnamed guide swipes a keycard in the door and opens it up. Inside, there are machines from top to bottom. Each one is whirring its own breath in and out with the churning of each of its parts. Giant plastic tubes line themselves up and circle back and forth, feeding long, fat strips of paper into dancing circles. We walk forward some more, past all the paper things, and find giant vats of bubbling goo. Large plastic oars attached to mechanical arms stir them in churning motions. It makes me seasick watching the substance wave in and out of focus as the ripples do the same.

"I hear we have some visitors today."

By now, I know this voice like the back of my hand, but my brain can't break away from the swirling goo vat in front of me. I'm pretty sure I know what this is. I'm pretty sure I'm staring at a vat of DMSO. The thought itself feels completely unreal. And yet, it's what makes complete sense.

"Good afternoon."

I turn around to see what I already know. It's the red-headed woman. The same one who was so annoyed while buying a cart full of metal tools, and the same one who guided us on the gallery tour. Now, this woman is staring at both of us, sizing me up and Stark down. I swallow, hoping her glasses are so thick her memory of us couldn't have penetrated through the lenses and burrowed into her head.

She wrinkles her nose and crosses her arms. "You," she says.

The single word is all I need to hear to know, she's got the memory of an elephant.

"And how exactly can I help you today?" Though she strings out the word "you" as if it were sandpaper in her throat she couldn't cough out.

Stark holds out his hand to shake hers. "Stark Landon, ma'am. It's a pleasure to formally meet you on your turf."

"Turf?" She coughs out this word, too.

"Sure. My turf is the craft store. Yours is here."

She nods. "Craft Your Pants. That's exactly where I remember seeing you. It's where I see all the people who think they know anything about art and yet couldn't name off any Monet painting without Googling it."

"Water Lilies, Poppies, and Irises."

While I'm busy trying to figure out why Stark is naming off flowers, I notice the corners of this lady's mouth pop upward in the smallest motion.

"And Davinci?"

"Easy, Mona Lisa."

Now I get it. He's naming off artwork.

She shakes her head at Stark. "That's too easy. Try something a little less... known by the banals."

Banals? As in common people? The offensiveness of her tone washes over me.

"Still easy. The Virgin of the Rocks and Ginerva de' Benci."

She gives him a knowing look, and yet she still wants to size him up. "Salvador Dali, but don't say The Persistence of Memory. Everyone already knows that." The disdain in her voice is almost completely gone.

Stark clears his throat as if he's about to recite a monologue. "Under the split in the retreating black cloud, the invisible scale of spring is oscillating in the fresh April sky."

Maybe the pine fumes are getting to me, but is Stark speaking a whole new language? What is this?

He continues, "On the highest mountain, the god of the snow, his dazzling head bent over the dizzy space of reflections.."

"Starts melting with desire in the vertical cataracts of the thaw annihilating himself loudly among the excremental cries of minerals!" The woman interrupts Stark with the same bizarre language. There's no way that entire thing is the name of a painting. Not even the craziest of artists would do that... would they?

"The Metamorphosis of Narcissus! I have underestimated you, boy. You're alright in my books. That is, if your hands can match your mouth." Her distaste is starting to slide back from view, and I'm starting to realize I'm happy being on the sidelines, being completely ignored by these artsy-smartsy people because there's no way I could contribute to this conversation in a way that would benefit any of us.

The corners of Stark's mouth turn up. He knows his knowledge is impressive, but I wonder what he feels about the second part of what she said. The part about him proving his worth with his actual talent. Because that's the part that makes me sweaty and unsure on his behalf.

"And how about you, Ms…" This woman lets her word dangle as she addresses me. So much for blending into the background.

"Olivia Landon." My full name sounds uncomfortable to my own ears, and yet it's what my mouth decided to give her. I suppose formality seems in place for introductions.

"Ah, Landon. So the two of you are siblings? Are you just as well versed as your brother, here?" I can smell the skepticism coming off her, and it's there for good reason.

"I'm sorry, ma'am. All of the artsy stuff is my brother here. He's clearly the star of this show."

"The star, huh? We'll see about that." Her entire tone has dropped with cynicism. That is, until she turns back to Stark to re-spark the conversation with him.

"So, let's see what you have up your sleeve, shall we?"

Stark and I exchange looks. What on earth is this woman talking about? Her words challenge him. Her eyes, I assume, are doing the same.

And judging by the way all the men in this room have very suddenly appeared from all corners of the factory to gather around us, everyone here is judging Stark. They enclose us in a circle, all their eyes facing us in the center as if they're about to participate in Stark's sacrifice. Or mine. I don't know if I got away with something or not, having already been passed off with judgment, but I'm a little terrified over what they're going to do next, especially if they decide Stark isn't worthy.

The woman in front of us claps her hands together. A signal, I suppose, because one man leaves his place in the circle and walks over to a finished roll of paper. He lifts up the free end, not yet secured down by tape or glue or plastic wrap for the public consumption. Then, he rips off a piece. It's almost perfectly sized to the squares of paper that come in the packaging. He must have experience judging the size of paper sheets with his own hands.

From there begins a little assembly line, or rather, assembly circle, as if each of these men have been here before. Their bodies know what to do as if they've been programmed to do it without question.

The man who ripped the paper hands it to another. He folds it, but just a small part at the top, not quite in half. Another man takes the paper and does the same, just a little further down from the first fold mark. A third man does the same, even further down on the paper.

A fourth man unfolds all the creases to flatten the paper out. He gives out a big grin as if his job is the most exciting out of all of them. I give him a "What the heck?" look back. Then, he passes it on to the next person in the circle.

This man holds the paper in one hand and pulls out a pencil from his pocket with the other. He holds the paper in a way that hides what he's doing from the rest of us— the circle of linen men and the three of us watching from the center.

The man next to him turns his back as an offering for a flat surface. The man with a pencil in hand accepts the offer, places the paper down on his surface, and starts his work. I think he's writing something. Or drawing. But his concentration is outstanding as all eyes focus on his dancing pencil, waiting to see what will come of it.

After a few minutes, he stops. The pencil drops back into his pocket and one of the folds goes back into place.

The paper gets passed again, and the next man does nearly the exact same thing, with a similar look of determination on his face. He folds the paper back on the next fold, and passes.

This continues a couple more rounds. Each time a new person is handed the paper, they make marks on it no one can see, then they fold the paper back so the next person doesn't even get a peek. The puffs and churns of the machinery around us provide the background music for this uninvited ceremony Stark and I have found ourselves in.

And now, the eyes shift. They all turn off the man who was last making marks on this communal paper, and they land on Stark. Each gaze is anxiously awaiting as the last man folds back the paper once more and hand delivers it to him. My eyes follow, also landing on Stark. I can feel the beads of sweat forming under my hair, and as much as I want to tap out the uncomfortable feeling, I watch him like a hawk. If there is a sacrifice about to happen, I'll do my best to jump into his place.

Cool as a cucumber, Stark is smiling. And not just a polite smile. He's enjoying this. He's truly enjoying being a part of whatever is happening. It's as if he knows exactly what's going on. And, it's as if he has been prepared his entire life.

His hand reaches into his back pocket, and when I realize what he's reaching for, I smile, too. I can't remember the last time I saw him hold a pencil, a crayon, or anything really, that would lead to his hands being put to work like they used to. It's been a long time since he's been prepared to challenge the inspiration that would show up at a moment's notice.

That's when I always saw him at his happiest, at his best. I'm reminded of why I clicked so well with Mills, too. I saw my brother in her. At least, the same fire of creativity. And, well, at least the fire he used to have. It's good to see a pencil in his hand now. I can almost feel the little spark ignite inside him after being out for so long.

With the same concentration as the men standing around us, Stark goes to work. Only, no one offers a back to him. He's using the palm of his free hand instead. The pink eraser dances ferociously in the air, but I can't see what the other end of the pencil is doing. Stark is too tall, and his cupped hand conceals anything from my angle of vision. But the way he bites down on his tongue and his eyes are darting around on what he's doing, I feel like he's been here before.

Not here, here. Not placed in the center of a circle of people staring at him. But mentally, here, where he's comfortably creating. And he understands whatever ritualistic game he's been charged with.

Another few not exactly silent minutes go by, and Stark slides his pencil back into its hiding place in his pocket. It's as if a giant weight is lifted from the room. The tension held within this circle goes limp as he holds out the paper he had been working on.

One last linen man breaks the circle to take it from him, and hand delivers it to the red-headed woman.

I can't help but to think, if Mills were here she'd make a comment about the overly generous trip that man had to make to deliver such a package. All four steps must have been strenuous for him.

The red-headed lady takes the paper and unfolds all the creases that were made and unmade by the hands of her minions. She forms her own creases in her forehead, taking in whatever it is in front of her. She scratches the top of her head, pulls a finger down to her chin. A cracked nail scratches at her skin there, too. When that same finger taps her nose, he nods. What starts as a tiny bob of her head morphs into enthusiastic acknowledgment.

"Yes, yes!" Her hand slaps the paper and holds it up into the air to show everyone.

Whatever I'm seeing, it doesn't make sense. It's bizarre, strange, just completely surreal. In fact, I'm pretty sure that's the kind of art it is. One man's head meets the slender neck of a giraffe, meets the body of a woman, meets the feet of a rabbit. Rabbit feet with a little rose off to the side.

As insane as that sounds, it all somehow works. I get it now; each person drew a piece of this photo without having known anything that was drawn before. Each section is drawn in a different style, and all incredible. Details pop off the page. Shadows create extra depth. Every weird molecule of this collaborative project makes sense as an artistic creation that could only be created by the hands of several minds. It's weird, and I like it. I wish Mills could be here to see it, and the proud look on Stark's face.

"Gentlemen, we have ourselves here a new member!"

The lump in my throat hardens up at this woman's words. What does she mean by *member*?

"I hope you like linen." She loops her arm through Stark's.

I just lost my brother to the same rabbit hole I lost my best friend down.

CHAPTER TWENTY-THREE

Noland

The skin on my arm feels like raw meat. Every time it throbs, blood pumps a little through the holes in my skin. The stinging stopped a while ago, now it's more like a burning heat. The little bit of special cream Doctor James left me in the cabinets helped. It really is magic, since it allowed me to numb my senses enough to hack away with every tool at my disposal.

My arm makes me think of tender, juicy steak. It's red like a fresh cut, and I bet if someone were to slab it in a pan, it would saute up nicely. I have to force myself to focus on a different taste in front of me.

My fork stabs inside the bag of gummy bears again, and I take another sour bite. It's what I found waiting for me in the kitchenette, so I know it's what I'm allowed to eat right now. On one hand, it'll sustain me for the moment. On the other hand, I'm way more interested in the artistry it took to create the raw meat sensation. It's a piece of art itself. I did well.

The way my canvas took to the variety of tools is so curious. It's not quite clay. Clay bends and folds and morphs into whatever you want. It turns out, skin is a little different. It's like taffy, harder than prepared clay, yet the first couple of layers are still soft enough to break into stickiness.

The first few punctures literally took my breath away. Every time my heart clicked another beat, the painful sting radiated to something completely new. Pain for art. Art for pain. I loved and hated it. And I love Doctor James even more for knowing me so completely that he left me what I needed.

And what's more interesting? Some of these tools made a bigger impression than others. I have a zigzag texture freckling my wrist. There's a track of little consummate v's running down to my elbow. The tool that creates a bubbly-bumpy texture was useless, though. It didn't do a thing to the first few layers of skin. Not until I pressed hard enough to feel the bruising start its cycle underneath. Maybe tomorrow it'll be more interesting. I'll wake up with little purpling bubbles on the side of my arm. It'll be exciting to see what tomorrow brings.

I've taken all the red that leaked out of the broken skin. Because I broke it on purpose, the red is appreciated. It means I'm experimenting the way I'm supposed to. But it's also annoying. It's getting in the way of my work, my purpose, to explore the possibilities.

My purpose. This is part of my purpose, right? That's why the tools were provided, right?

I take another look at my artwork. Of course it is. This is all part of the process, testing the waters and pushing the limits. Finding new inspirational creativity on mediums that haven't been played with yet by the artist himself. By me. I'm convinced that's exactly what The Dignitary expects from us. And looking at the way my self-canvas has reacted, I can feel excitement bubble up underneath my skin. It's just like the purpling bruises that will show up tomorrow. It's there, just ready to erupt to the surface for everyone to see. I cannot wait to see the reactions to both of them.

I wonder what everyone else is doing. All the other red Circle members who walked into their rooms to find the same spread. I bet some started to test with some of the softer tools, but lost their guts when they realized the hierarchy of experimentation was going to mean biting back their disgust. I bet others might have decided to use a more conventional canvas. Something already in the room, like the wooden table or the fabric in their bedspread.

But I bet Mills has a matching arm to mine. She's always been so inquisitive and willing. I imagine her curiosity ran wild like mine. I have no doubt she's sitting in her room right now, mirroring my seat at the table. Both of us admiring our artwork, and she, ready to compare it to mine and show it off to the world. She's always been above everyone else around her. All the students, all the artists, and now all the Circle members.

Knock, knock, knock.

The last time I thought someone knocked on my door, I was left disappointed. It's been quiet next door ever since, but I know better than to run and answer it like the fool I was last time. So I quietly walk my way to the wall that meets up with room number one and press my ear against it. One second passes, then two. I wait a little longer and then, *knock, knock, knock.*

Only it's not coming from the room next door. Nothing is coming from Number One. It's deadly quiet over there. Ghostly, even. It makes my heart jolt.

Knock, knock, knock.

It *is* my door. There really is someone there. And since everything is lining up to be exactly as I hope for, I know exactly who it is.

I race to answer it. My bloody hand that was just hard at work reaches for the doorknob and instantaneously twists it. Little droplets stain my wristband, but even the smeared handprint I leave behind feels like artwork. Maybe I could play with that later. A little finger painting on the walls and furniture. I may need some more of the magic serum to have enough, though. When the door swings open, I'm greeted with a grinning Doctor James. I'm sure my expression matches his. It might even be more exaggerated.

"Doctor James, how are you?" I can't help my words jumping out. My eyes jump, too. They scan him head to foot to see if he has the same little pill bottle he gave the woman in room number one.

"Noland Elsinger, I am doing well. I hope the same is for you?"

I see it. My eyes bounce from his hand to his eyes. I see the bottle with a single pill I believe is jingling around inside of it. And I want to grab at it without permission. Patience. Patience. Patience.

"Absolutely well, Doctor James. So glad to see you." The tips of my toes want to bounce on themselves. If the woman next door was able to get whatever it is in that bottle, special, just for The Circle, then I should get it and gobble it up, too. I hold my body still. This is my chance and I don't want to blow it. Patience.

"So good to hear that, Noland. I can see you found the gifts left on the table for you." He indicates my arm, and his expression is the proof that this is my home. I am in a place where people understand me and the tests of creativity I choose to create. His lips pull past his teeth, and his pride radiates from them.

I acknowledge this with my own grin. "They are quite the experiment. Thank you very much."

"Now, Noland, you know it's not my doing. I'm just happy to be here to assist The Society with the best care I can."

We stand in silence for a few moments. I know the kind of care he's going to give me, I'm just waiting for him to hand it over with instructions. So I can transfer and ascend, gain the clarity I've been craving, and finally *finally* meet Dali da Monet where It or She or They or whoever it is will guide me into the realm of enlightenment and imagination. As much as I'd like greediness to get me there — I suck in a breath and keep it hostage in my lungs — I know a few more moments of patience is what will open the gateway doors.

Exhale. Slowly.

A shuffle of my foot and a gaze at his hand, and the pill bottle is a few inches closer.

Exhale some more.

"Speaking of," Doctor James finally starts to speak again, "I have this for you." The glorious bottle. It's right in my eyesight, inches away from my face, ready for me to take.

Release the rest of the air and inhale again because it's here, it's here, it's finally here.

Grab isn't exactly the word I'd use. It's more like seeing his gesture activated a magnet in my hand and the bottle instantly and magically ended up in my grip. I explore the label on it. It doesn't say much. It's just a plain white label that says Enlightenment Pill in small black letters. Though, one of my artistic fingerprints covers the letters. But that's enough to mean the entire world.

I thank Doctor James. He's always had the best interest of every Memento Mori member at heart, and it's all led up to this. Before he can even give me any directions, the door closes on him. I'm an adult. I can figure out any kind of instructions on my own.

Breathe, Noland.

The door feels cool on my back as I slide down to the floor. I rake one hand through the plush carpet fibers. The other one jiggles the enlightenment pill bottle.

Enlightenment pill. Could it be so easy?

My hand moves from the carpet to the top of the bottle. It pushes down and twists, opens. A white oval pill stares back at me. It falls into the palm of my hand when I tip the bottle over. It's smaller than it looked at the bottom of the bottle. It's the size of a mint, really. A finger pokes at it and it doesn't move, just sits there unassuming.

But most important things are.

I pinch the pill between two fingers and feel its smooth casing. Within my touch, it slowly turns from white to red. Like my hand. Like my arm and my art. Like the paint that splattered across my chest to deem me important enough to be in The Circle. I give it a gentle squeeze. The casing bounces back, which tells me the inside is a powder, not gel. Once in my system, it'll take a few minutes. That's it. Maybe five minutes maximum. Five minutes and I'll officially wake up in the next realm.

I just wish Mills could be right here next to me, so we could cheer with our own red pills, set them down our individual hatches, and wake up arm in arm, enlightened, knowledgeable, and better than we have ever been.

Again, patience. I remind myself that patience is necessary. I've held myself back so far, a little more waiting won't kill me. Once this little bit of enlightenment is in my system, I'll have everything I've ever wanted.

Including Mills in my arms. By my side. For all of our second eternity.

That's where I land my thoughts. My mind blocks out everything else as it locks onto the feeling of Emily Ellis's hair, smile, her skin.

Down the hatch the red pill goes. No water necessary. It gets a little sticky in my throat, so I swallow again to force the metallic taste down. I can feel it dissolve and break, understanding spreading throughout my system.

I'll close my eyes for now. In a little bit, I'll open them up and she'll be by my side, ready and willing to be mine forever.

CHAPTER TWENTY-FOUR

Mills

There is a lot of pride inside of this lump of clay. My cupped hands hold onto a muddy red butterfly with two large wings that span out on either side, stretching their freedom. It's exactly how I feel — able to create anything, anything at all. No judgments. No restrictions. Only support for creative exploration. Because that's how we become enlightened on the truths and possibilities. Playing with what we have in front of us and stretching our limits until they break down and build up again.

I tried hard, really. I wanted to make something amazing out of a little lump of clay, prove to everyone including myself that I really am the artist I want to be. That I can create anything worth knowing with my hands.

But as we all know, good intentions only get us so far. The wings of this butterfly aren't the way they should be. If only I could keep these wings from falling over. Their own weight keeps them drooping down, flaccidly falling into muddy little blobs. But I use my free fingers to keep them from falling off and falling apart altogether. That's what my hands are good at - keeping the limp alive.

After getting to know Iris and the society, I now know exactly why Noland has brought me here. My talent. That's why I was painted red, separated from the sad blue and straight into The Circle where we'll get the chance to become enlightened artists, just like our artistic ancestors were.

This is where that happens. And I'm given the opportunity to explore all of that.

With my *talent*.

I feel just as free as my butterfly, with the ability to allow myself in and out of the main building, and straight up to the floor where my room is. As I step off the stairs to the third floor, I take a look at the locked door to the side of me. Behind it is the blue side, the sad side. The side where so-called artists will have a different meaning of existence, a different purpose of life, and it does not include going onto the next realm.

I know, I know. I sound pretty elitist. But, really, I'm kind of sad for them. There's a piece of me who wants to grab Iris and shake her, asking why there can't be enough room for *all* of us in The Circle.

I mean, can't circles be bigger? And the bigger the circle, the stronger it is?

But that's why she's The Dignitary and I'm just me. She's heard the voices of Dali da Monet, so she knows better. She definitely understands more, and there's definitely more I need to learn.

Through the glass window in the door, I see a familiar face. Zak. My heart does a little flutter thing, both excited to see him and terrified to watch him through the separation of glass between us. Does he really deserve to be left behind?

Balancing the clay butterfly in one hand, I use the other to tap my knuckles on the glass. At first, he doesn't notice anything. He's just stretching his arms in the hall, standing in one place as if he was designed to root on the spot. Then, I rap my knuckles on the glass again. A little harder, a lot noisier. That's what gets his attention.

A brief look of confusion washes over him, but a moment later, it's replaced with recognition. His eyebrows lift up as do the corners of his mouth, and his hand is waving wildly in the air. A blue wristband dangles as he waves. He's an adorable boy who can't contain his innocent greeting. It almost breaks my heart that he won't be able to carry that on to whatever is waiting for us next. Well, whatever is waiting for *some* of us.

Then Zak does something unexpected. He runs. He runs straight toward me, straight toward the door. From this little window, I can see the enthusiasm in every freckle on his face. His arms are flying in every direction, and his entire body is lit up like a firework that will explode if I don't help him release some of that excitement first.

Now that I see him like this, I'm not sure if I'm supposed to talk to him. My hands hold onto my butterfly, wondering what the rules actually are, or if there are any at all. I think back to the instructions we were given. I don't think we were told not to communicate with anyone in blue. Perhaps my subconscious made that rule up since I know in my heart of hearts we were being separated for a reason. And the physical separation must have significance, so wouldn't an emotional separation be beneficial, too?

But then, Zak does something else unexpected. He lifts up his keycard so I can see it. It has a number seven on it, just like mine. The only difference is that his seven looks glossy and new, which makes my scuffed card look sad and used.

I read the words, "Back up," on his lips, so I take a step back and his shiny keycard disappears out of my view.

There's a hiss and a click and… the door opens.

It opens?

Weren't we told we couldn't go past this door? There isn't even a card scanner on my side, so even if mine would open a door to the sad blue area, there isn't a place to try.

He opens it up and steps over the threshold to embrace me with a hug.

"Zak! This is a pleasant surprise. How are you?"

"Mills! I'm fantastic. Can you even believe these rooms? The comfort? The food?"

I give him a little laugh. "Did you get chicken nuggets, too?"

He laughs back. "Chicken nuggets? Mills, the spread was so much better than that! Fresh fruit and veggies, roasted chicken, four different types of cheeses with salted crackers."

Roasted chicken and fresh vegetables? Maybe I should have been complaining about more than dino nuggies.

"What's that in your hand?" He pulls back from me to examine my poor sagging butterfly, now a little more squished than before.

"Oh, this is just a little clay piece I made." I lift the butterfly up for him to see it better and adjust the wings so they stand up again.

His smile feels sympathetic. "I'm so glad you got to explore a little. I hear not everyone had the chance to do so with clay."

I nod, though I don't really understand what that means. I assumed everyone had the chance to do the same thing. I assumed Iris went around delivering little bundles of clay to go with the tools we had. But maybe not. Maybe not everyone had the chance to experiment with the gifts, yet.

"You know, I don't think I'm supposed to tell you this, Mills." He's whispering now, and the amount of enthusiasm I feel seeping out of his pores is less than when he first entered this part of the floor. He must be holding some of it back. "But I'm too excited not to. You've been so kind to me and everything, I can't keep secrets from you now. At least not this one."

"Zak?"

I look through the little window again. At first, I thought the hall behind it looked just like the one I live in. The same similar paintings on the wall, the same line of rooms, curving along the hallway. But now that I'm looking again, I realize, it's not the same at all. The paintings are bigger, and set in gold frames. The doors are freshly painted, no faded spots where anyone might have scuffed on while passing. Even the floor looks like it's had a fresh wax. Each tiny detail tells me that the two sections of this floor aren't treated the same, which has me wondering, why does my door have scuff marks on it? And what secret is Zak so excited to share when he's not supposed to?

"Mills, this place. We both know this isn't your average art camp, right?" His eyes are sparkling, but his mouth stays serious. "Like, we're given the space and freedom to do what we want, create what we want, with the supplies we're given, right?"

I nod; yes, we know this.

"Well, some of the supplies are… unique." He gulps at his tiny pause and I can see his pupils dilate.

I make a mental list of the supplies I've been given. Paper, paste, paints, sculpting tools, and clay. I nod as if I understand his meaning, but the reality is, nothing here is too unique. Maybe it's made me stretch my abilities a little, but that's just because I'm a painter at heart. But that doesn't mean I can't do other things. Perhaps Zak means that he's been pushing his limits outside of his choice of medium, too.

Then, Zak bites his lip, and gets closer in a low voice. "Dali de Monet came to me last night."

Okay, *this* is unique. This is unheard of. I mean, I know everyone wants to have their chance to hear the collective voices, but my understanding is that hardly anyone has heard Dali de Monet speak to them directly. Noland said he experienced the connection once, but it was physical. He didn't hear any voice or message or anything like that. Only The Dignitary holds conversations with the ultimate ancestral being. I can't imagine any of the recruits getting anywhere near that kind of experience, especially one of the sad blue recruits who aren't even part of The Circle at all.

"They told me that you were going to be a part of my success."

Excuse me, huh? Does this mean that his purpose and mine are connected? Is he somehow going to help me into the next realm?

"They told me we're connected, and that your purpose will unlock the next realm for me."

I shake my head. No; that's not right. "Zak, I think you're mistaken. I…"

And that's when I hear footsteps behind me. Zak's face falls. "I can't say anymore," he whispers at me, and he waves goodbye with concerned eyes. In a hurry, he leaves down the stairway. I guess because he can't use his keycard to go back to the sad blue side. Again, there's not a scan box to even try.

I turn to the sound of footsteps. There, two men in linen, the No Names as I've learned them to be, are rolling a stretcher down the hall. They stop in front of room number two. One scans his card to let both of themselves in. For a few silent moments, I wonder what's happening behind the door. What they might be delivering. Or maybe retrieving.

The door opens again, and out come the two men.

And a third. On the stretcher. A familiar vacant face stares back at me.

The nose that always pointed in my direction. The dark hair that used to sweep over his face, and the eyes that always drank me in, from head to tail to the tips of my fingers every time I picked up a paintbrush.

It's Noland, and he's being wheeled out of his room like a death patient in a hospital ward. Maybe they're bringing him to Doctor James. Maybe he needs the kind of care only a doctor can give.

His left arm drops lifelessly from the stretcher. Each finger on his hand is a fat worm, out to sun itself into lifelessness. Part of me wants to run to it and grab it. I want to know if it still holds any warmth. I want to know if his fingers still feel the same laced through mine. Then, one of the No Names flops it back on the metal surface. The way it lays there, clamming up, I know I don't have to touch it at all to know it'll never be the same again.

Because it's not just his hand. It's his wrist and arm, too. All I can see is little marks all over the skin. They're the same ones I created to dot and texture the butterfly in my hand. I look down on it. I was excited to have clay to play with. I wanted to know what each tool could do. I thought I was getting ready for another judgment. Maybe something similar to the gallery. Or maybe something more small-scale, out of the public's eye. Now, I'm not so sure what I was preparing for.

A hiss alerts me to turn my head again. The door to the blue side opens up and I quickly make my way to the stair corridor out of sight. I don't want to be caught being a Peeping Tom at Noland's body, not when it was meant for something so much better than this.

From here, I can see a third No Name prop open the door and allow the others to roll in. I can't see his face, just a dark hand jutting out to help Noland's body through the doorway. That's when it hits me. That's not a stretcher. That's a gurney.

I think the man who helped me to see my *talent* is dead.

CHAPTER TWENTY-FIVE

Stark

Majestic corpse. I can't believe this operation judged me based on a child's art game, something I used to do for fun when I kept a pencil in my pocket and friends by my side. It's a good thing I decided to bring one with me today. Boyscout motto, always be prepared, and all that. And if I'm being honest, it was fun. I enjoyed drawing again. It makes me forget why I ever put down the pencil in the first place. I suppose that's another story for another day.

Had I come across a place who did this kind of thing on the regular back then, I probably would have jumped head first into coming here without ever looking back. It makes total sense why someone could end up here.

No doubt, that was the fear I saw in Livvy's face when I handed her my keys and told her goodbye. I told her to go home without looking back. I don't want her hanging around to see what it might take from here. I don't even know if she'd survive if she had stuck around to find out. I don't think she would.

We'll get back in touch. I know we will. She may not be able to throw out the names of Dali's paintings, but she's smart. She'll find a way to peek in, and I'll find a way to help her see. I trust she'll do her part on the other side while I do mine in here.

Until then, I'm going to chill in these linen clothes and follow along to what I'm told. It can't be too hard to find Mills in this place. Not if I play their game to find her.

My first assignment is the blue floor. If I'm being honest, it's surprising. I figured I'd be somewhere in the factory or on bathroom duty. But they said the real test of strength and promise was up here.

If I fail, I'm out. Not as in out of the commune I weaseled myself into. Out as is done. Dead. Gone from this earth. They're not even promising me some bullshit excuse of enlightenment. I'll be killed off and fed to the factory machines to power them up.

So this assignment is do or die. There's no in-between. And if I do, then I'm in. I'll have proved my allegiance.

Based on the number of security swipes I need to buzz myself through, I've gathered that blue is one of the highest ranks. Not *the* highest. Not as high as the red-headed Dignitary herself, but the people on this floor are definitely well-revered.

Which means if I screw this up, then I screw up royally. Jumping straight into this level of things means I've been pushed into Shitt's Creek without a paddle. So I need to swim or I'll drown in the crap around me.

And possibly, so will Mills. I can't let that happen. I've gotten this far. I need to keep riding the wave and go further.

What's odd is that this building is circular, yet there are two doors that separate half the floor, both with security keypads I need to swipe to enter. I don't know how the floors above me look, but this isn't like the free circle on the floors below where you could walk in the same direction over and over and continue to pass the same doors each time. This feels secluded, purposeful. Like there's something on the other side I need to see.

And the truth is? It's part of my assignment to figure out. I pass up a few doors that remind me of the dorms the few times I've visited Livvy. Only, there's a single door that's open and a peek inside tells me this is nowhere near dorm living. This is much nicer. The furniture is clean, the walls are freshly painted, and everything inside appears to be new.

No hand-me-downs and thrift store furniture here. Though there's one thing propped up in the frame of this door, and it catches my eye just enough to pause in my step. A paper mâché machete. A paper machete.

Though the paint marks on it don't say anything to me, there's something about the build of it that does. The way the handle curves and the blade points organically, I feel like I know the artist who created it. And even though it's not perfect, I can't think of anyone else who could have made it. I wish I could touch it so I could be sure that Mills's hands created this. But I can't.

How I'd love to hold it, feel its weight. How I'd love to carry it down the hall and wield it as a weapon. I'd slash away at all the villains, find Mills, and free us out of this place like a knight in shining armor.

But I'm no knight. And a paper machete isn't going to slash away the demons that prowl these halls.

I keep moving, hoping for any sign of Mills. Preferably, Mills herself. But it's not like I can let myself into any of these rooms in front of me to go poking around. If I catch the wrong person off guard and deviate from the assignment, I'm out of here.

And we all know what out of here means.

So no deviating. Not until I have a plan. Not until I find Mills and figure out how we're going to get her out of here.

The door I need is in front of me. The one that leads to the other half of this floor. My entire assignment is to open it up and let in the other No Names. That's it. I don't touch anything. I don't say anything.

That's what they call us, the men in linen jumpsuits, No Names. They don't even hide the fact that we don't matter. And yet, they've utterly convinced each one of the other men that they do. Somehow, they've found every person in a hundred-mile radius who feels lost enough and with a big enough need of people who understand their art. Then, they sucked them in and fed them stories about how important their presence is. That's when they stripped them of the one thing that matters — their identity.

My keycard is attached to a lanyard in my pocket. When I pull it out, it feels like a leash I've chosen to attach myself to. I lift it up to scan the door open. It hisses and clicks, and when I ease it open, a flash of linen skirts away. And with it, a familiar streak of blonde. A lump catches in my throat, and even though I try to swallow it down, it stays painfully there. A reminder that the impossible is happening right in front of me.

It's Mills.

And if she's darting away into hiding, then she's not the Mills I remember. The Mills I remember would have slapped me on the shoulder and smartmouthed her way out of this place.

There are a lot of things that can change a person. Trauma, sadness, isolation. But I imagine a place like this would change a person just as quickly. Perhaps permanently. The thought makes me angry. How dare they take away the pieces of Emily Ellis that make her, her.

I force my body to stay where it is. All but my arm which swings the door open the rest of the way. That's because she's not my assignment. She's not what I'm told to wait for. What I'm waiting for is something else entirely.

It's the two men rolling a body my way. I open the door to them. And even though the body is fresh, its blank face still flush and its eyes not yet clouded over, I swear I can smell death seeping off of it.

I was told there would be unique supplies for those on the blue side, arriving on a rolled out platter. This is it. This is the supplies. Those on the The Circle side are using *bodies as supplies*. And those on the other side — the red side — will become their supplies one by one.

As they slide through the doorway, I force a smile to thank them for their duty. I clench my teeth and allow them to roll past. And even when the dead hand brushes up against me, I stay statue still with a look of false delightfulness on my face. This is my assignment.

But Mills? She's my inevitability.

A REVIEW REQUEST

Thank you so much for dedicating some of your time to get to know the characters who have been with me for so long. If you enjoyed this book, please take a few minutes to rate and review Paint by Murders on Goodreads or Amazon.

Even a few words help others decide if this is the book meant for them.

***

Your Book is Lonely!

Please consider adding a few friends on your shelf!

<u>Emily Ellis Thrillers</u>
Paint by Murders
Paper Machete
Majestic Corpse

<u>Other Books by Amanda Jaeger</u>
The Fallen in Soura Heights
BreathTaken

ABOUT THE AUTHOR

Amanda Jaeger: Murderino mom of two, professional word nerd by day and author by trade.

She's the wife of her college sweetheart, and the mother of two spitfire girls, but she's also been a sign language interpreter, transcriptionist, and a book slinger. Working with words isn't her job, it's her career.

Thank goodness writing thrillers come naturally to her.

Amanda refuses to start her day without the perfect cup of coffee and a cuddle with her poodles. She also wants to let you know that poodles aren't as prissy as they seem, and they are, in fact, made of teeth, nails, and heads as hard as steel.

Residing in Virginia, you can bet on Amanda listening to true crime podcasts, watching cold case documentaries, and playing with her kids. (Not simultaneously).

And even though Amanda kinda sucks at keeping up with social media trends, she loves connecting one-on-one with readers.

You can connect with Amanda:
Text "ThrillerRead" to: (844) 495-1120

ACKNOWLEDGMENTS

Holy crap I hope I don't forget anyone. It takes a village, y'all. It's just as true for paperback babies as it is for the real-life sticky ones. (And yes, kids are sticky.) So please bear with me and if you made it this far in this book, then keep on reading. These are my village to have helped make this trilogy the crazy semi-beast it is.

Before I head into it, let me clear the air that ALL MISTAKES ARE MIIIINE.

Hey YOU, yes you. The person reading this. Thank YOU. You're the reason why I write and continue to write. The characters and stories may start with me, but you're what keep them alive for much, much longer.

To the real-life Mariëtte who really is one of those people who you never know what's hidden beneath the surface. Thank you for being my number 1 Alpha. You're always there to help me find the gaps when my brain is fried. And without you, I'd probably get every forensic scene 1,000% wrong.

To allllll the betas: Anna, Danielle, Jamie, Carmen, and Sam. Thank you for helping me refine the details, close the gaps even further, and sometimes rearranging the cluster in my head to make more sense on paper.

The Thriller Babes: You know who you are. Out of the entire writers' community, you are the pillar that keeps me standing when the frustrations run high. Your help, guidance, expertise, and self-deprecating memes are everything I ever wanted in a peer mentorship. Thank you!

My editor, Genevieve… good grief I couldn't do this without you. Thank you so much for helping me clean things up as I learn and relearn what the heck grammar is all about. (You'd think as an English major I would have had some kind of grammar class… but nah.)

Troy! You're stuck with me. Forever. Deal with it. Thank you for always knowing exactly how to take my insane descriptions and translate them into visuals. I know they say "Don't judge a book by its cover," but we all know that's the first thing people judge a book by. Your cover designs make my first impressions better.

To my husband, Michael, for always being supportive of my crazy writing "hobby" (slash work slash obsession). Because of you, I have the time, space, and love to actually create the stories that keep me up all night.

My kids, who keep asking what the heck I'm writing about but aren't allowed to yet read it. I know you two have snuck a few peeks over my shoulder. I'm not mad, but I'll definitely understand if you need therapy later. Love you to pieces.

And the rest of my family who continue to be supportive both loudly and quietly. Thank you for reading when you want, loving me even when you don't want to read it, and smiling when I talk to much about it. THANK YOU FOR BEING YOU.